Hawkes Harbor

S. E. Hinton

Hawkes Harbor

A Tom Doherty Associates Book

NEW YORK

HAWKES HARBOR

Book design by Mary A. Wirth

A Tor Book
Published by Tom Doherty Associates, LLC
175 Fifth Avenue
New York, NY 10010

www.tor.com

Tor® is a registered trademark of Tom Doherty Associates, LLC.

Library of Congress Cataloging-in-Publication Data

Hinton, S. E.
    Hawkes Harbor / S.E. Hinton.—1st ed.
      p.   cm.
    "A Tom Doherty Associates book."
    ISBN 0-765-30563-1 (hc) (acid-free paper)
    EAN 978-0765-30563-3 (hc)
    ISBN 0-765-31306-5 (first international trade paperback edition)
    EAN 978-0765-31306-5 (first international trade paperback edition)
    1. Illegitimate children—Fiction.   2. Seaside resorts—Fiction.
3. Murderers—Fiction.   4. Monsters—Fiction.   5. Delaware—Fiction.
6. Orphans—Fiction.   I. Title.

PS3558.I548H39   2004
813'.54—dc22

                                                            2004048049

First Edition: September 2004

Printed in the United States of America

0 9 8 7 6 5 4 3 2 1

David, one more time

Hawkes Harbor

Prologue

The boy sat in the open window and watched the baseball game in the vacant lot across the street.

He should be down there, playing, he thought. Not stuck in here.

He'd earned the right to play. He was small for eight years old, but he'd shown them he was fast, with fighting. He'd shown them he was tough, agile, and no patsy, fighting.

They called him a bastard and he'd shown them he didn't care, by not crying. After all, truth was truth.

Now he was going to have to go somewhere else and show a whole new group of kids.

Well, if that was what it took . . .

He tried to ignore the conversation going on behind him in the now-empty apartment. Father Nolan and the strange nun were looking over Jamie's few possessions.

"This is all?"

"The girl was a stenographer. They hardly accumulate wealth." Father Nolan's voice was dry.

"The boy—conceived in adultery, born in sin—he'll need special supervision. The sins of the father . . ."

"Sister, I knew the boy's father. Both he and the mother were in my parish. He was a good, decent boy, killed in the Pacific in defense of his country. He meant to marry the girl, I know it. Wartimes aren't like other times."

Father Nolan knew he had been too lenient with his parish during the war, but life had been harsh enough then . . . surely any expression of love . . .

"Sin is sin. Well, is this everything?" Her voice was brisk, businesslike.

"Yes." Father Nolan's heart sank. He had dreaded this moment for a week now, since the visit that confirmed his worst fears—the girl wasn't sick but dying. And she was frantic at leaving Jamie.

"Jamie. Come here, lad."

Sighing, Jamie left the window. Time to go with Father Nolan. Jamie had known the tall, white-haired priest all his life, and he was tired of staying with the Carters next door. They were tired of him, too, Mrs. Carter had informed him.

"It was just the Christian thing to do," she said, "while

Colleen was in the hospital. And it certainly isn't permanent . . ."

Father Nolan knelt, put his hands on Jamie's shoulders. "It's time to go with Sister Mary Joseph now. You'll be with other boys who have no parents, well-looked after, you'll go to school."

Jamie looked from the sad dark eyes to the impatiently waiting nun. What was happening? Father Nolan was supposed look after him now.

"But you promised Colleen *you'd* take care of me," Jamie wanted to say—he'd been there, he had heard. His mother had whispered, "Take care of Jamie," and Father Nolan whispered, "Yes."

And now the priest was handing him over to this stranger.

But Jamie's throat tightened. He would not cry again. He was through with that. He wouldn't cry again, ever.

She had gone and died on him. After all the fights he'd had because of her—because he had no dad—and she too, had promised him, "I won't leave you, Jamie."

Jamie stood stunned, trying to adjust to his second great betrayal that week. The two people he trusted most had lied to him.

Father Nolan straightened. The nuns had a reputation for strictness, but surely they'd be kind to him. Jamie was an unusually appealing little boy, with his bright wheat-colored hair, his large golden-hazel eyes; very solemn for his age, quiet, but when he smiled it broke your heart, Father Nolan thought . . . he got that from his mother.

Perhaps it would do him good, Father Nolan tried to reason. The boy could use a little discipline—his mother had spoiled him . . . trying to make it up to him. . . .

"What's this?" the nun said sharply.

She pulled at the chain around Jamie's neck, lifted it and the crucifix over his head.

"Sister!" Father Nolan said sharply. "There's no need for such roughness!"

"T-t-that's m-mine," Jamie choked out, his first stammer. He'd rather do that than cry.

His mother had hung it around his neck the last time he saw her.

"Wear it always and remember to say your prayers, Jamie. Ask our dear Lord to protect you. It's our hope of heaven, Jamie."

He didn't want to wear it—necklaces were for girls—but he'd hid it in his shirt to please her.

"You give it b-b-back!"

The nun turned the crucifix in the sun.

Small but heavy. Solid gold. Set with a diamond and three rubies.

"Hardly a toy for a child," she said, "and when you think about how much the orphanage needs . . ."

"Sister, it was the father's grandmother's—surely it belongs to the boy."

"It is not only traditional but necessary that all valuables be donated to the orphanage. Charities must always be accepting of any gift the Lord provides."

She put the chain and crucifix in her small bag. Jamie watched it disappear forever.

Father Nolan put his hand on Jamie's head. "You must be a good boy now. And mind your temper."

Father Nolan knew the boy's reputation for fighting—if Jamie hadn't been bullied, he often thought, he would not have behaved so—

The sailor lad, the father, had been one of the kindest boys he'd known.

"He'll be good, all right. We'll see to that," the nun said firmly.

Jamie looked straight ahead, ignoring both, staggering only a little when the nun thrust his bags at him.

He followed her without a word. Never once looked back.

He'd lost his hope of heaven.

Interview

Terrace View Asylum, Delaware
JANUARY 1967

"So, Jamie, you've had a few weeks to adjust to Terrace View. How do you like it so far?"

Dr. McDevitt looked at the young man seated in front of his desk. A small, well-built young man who might have been handsome had it not been for his gauntness, the listlessness of his posture, the shadows around his shifting eyes.

He kept wringing his hands together.

"It's okay," Jamie answered, not looking up.

Dr. McDevitt wasn't insulted at Jamie's shrug, implying a

well-run sanitarium wasn't any better than that state institutional hellhole, Eastern State, where he'd been for the last few months. Right now the young man probably couldn't tell one place from another. After all, he only recently could remember his name. And the brutal way he had been transferred here . . . Dr. McDevitt was sure it had set his progress back for weeks.

"Grenville Hawkes asked that you be placed here. Do you remember Grenville Hawkes?"

Jamie shook his head.

"You used to work for him—he wanted to make sure you received the best treatment. Do you remember working for Grenville Hawkes, back in Hawkes Harbor?"

Dr. McDevitt thought he discerned a small flinch in Jamie's posture, but there was no change in tone, as he said, "No."

Dr. McDevitt glanced across the scanty medical report. Some doctor from Eastern State, who forgot to sign his name, had made a note that this was one of the worst cases of depression he'd ever tried to treat—it was no doubt a major cause of the amnesia. In the beginning, the patient would wake having no memory of the day before, would literally forget his own name by afternoon. Some memory of his early life was now returning, the report stated.

Not much to go on, but Eastern State was a place of housing, not treatment.

Dr. McDevitt wished he had more background. Jamie had been transferred here abruptly, at the insistence of Louisa Kahne. Her grandfather Johnas Kahne had founded and still technically ruled Terrace View. (The commonly held view, and joke, was that the esteemed Dr. Kahne wanted to make sure his progeny had a place to live; and out of all his swarm of eccentric descendants, this granddaughter was perhaps the most likely candidate.)

"Money is no problem," Louisa had insisted when she called demanding a room. "A favor for a friend of mine, Grenville Hawkes. Jamie'll be arriving some day this week. Yes, yes, I know, you're not accustomed to patients from the criminally insane ward at Eastern State, but crazy is crazy, after all."

No other instructions. Only a short note, and the deposit from Grenville Hawkes, followed in the mail.

Dr. McDevitt had decided to treat him on his own. There were no other instructions, recommendations. Apparently his bene-factors were content if he'd just sit here, abandoned like some stray dropped off at a shelter. Jamie had seemed to respond to Dr. McDevitt well and from the first. . . .

Dr. McDevitt still remembered the horrible beginning of Jamie Sommers's stay at Terrace View. It had gone to his heart when the young man turned to him.

"Dr. McDevitt, the new patient's here. James Sommers."

"Is Miss Kahne showing him to his room?"

"No, Miss Kahne's not with him. He's in a police car. He won't get out. And the officer is getting threatening."

Dr. McDevitt ran outside with Nurse Whiting. Yes, it was a police car. And an officer trying to talk sports with Lee. The attendant looked grim. No one without compassion was allowed to work at Terrace View.

"Hey, you want to get this nutcase outta my patrol car?" was the officer's greeting to the doctor. "I can't get Nurse Nancy here to help haul him."

Dr. McDevitt went to the car. The back doors were open, no one visible. He leaned in. Jamie Sommers was seated on the floor, head down. Dear God, they'd put him in a straitjacket. There were shackles on his ankles. There was no mention of violence on his hospital record.

"Mr. Sommers," he said.

Jamie slowly raised his head. Young, thin, unshaven, dirty. And madness in his eyes.

"If you'll let me help you out, I'll remove your restraints. I'm sure they must be painful."

The man was still recovering from some very serious physical injuries. Louisa had attempted to gloss over that fact, but Jamie's medical records had preceded his arrival.

"Captain Harvard?" Jamie said uncertainly. He looked puzzled, hopeful.

"May I help you?"

"Sure," Jamie said. It was the last time he spoke for several days.

He was improving, now. He slept on his bed, not under it. He startled far too easily, but jumped, no longer screamed. Still suffered from night terrors. He was terrified of most of the attendants (Eastern State could take credit for a lot of that, the doctor suspected) but let Nurse Whiting trim his hair. He was settled enough in his new surroundings for a first session.

Dr. McDevitt looked over the report once more.

Interesting case, a kind they rarely got at Terrace View. A criminal, apparently (Dr. McDevitt had a copy of Jamie's police record as well as his medical reports), shot during a suspected kidnapping.

Dr. McDevitt winced as he read about the three bullets being surgically removed—God knew what kind of treatment Jamie'd received after leaving Hawkes Harbor Hospital for Eastern State. The doctor had heard stories about the infirmary there.

"Well, Jamie, my records show you are twenty-five years of age?"

"Sounds right."

"Raised in St. Catherine's Orphanage, Bronx, attended Billingsworth High, Bronx, three years in the navy . . ."

Dr. McDevitt paused—but Jamie didn't confirm any of it. Eastern State had suggested Jamie's memory of his early life was returning, but Jamie had given no indication of this other than knowing his name.

He watched with interest as Jamie's eyes went to the window. Dr. McDevitt had chosen this time of day for the interview with reason.

Jamie shifted in his chair, looked around for a clock, gripped his hands together, wiped them on his pants.

Twenty-five. Dr. McDevitt would have guessed him slightly older—sun had burned lines into his face, pain had stamped dark circles under his eyes.

"Did you like the navy?"

"Liked getting my third mate's papers. They're real handy."

"It gives no reason for your early discharge."

"I got sick of taking orders."

"There's no report of any discipline problem on your previous hospital record."

"Don't want no trouble." Jamie slumped down again. His eyes went back to the window. He swallowed.

"You know what time it is?" he asked.

"Sixish. Your former employer, Mr. Hawkes, gave us a glowing report, and assured us he still believed you innocent of any wrongdoing."

Jamie looked confused.

"I'm referring to your . . . mishap with the Hawkes Harbor police."

"I didn't hurt anybody." Jamie's voice rose. "I know he shot me, but he didn't need to, I wasn't hurting anybody."

"It's all right, Jamie," Dr. McDevitt said. "All criminal charges have been dropped."

There had been no evidence with which to charge him.

In fact, when the doctor looked at the report, his first thought was to wonder why the lawman had thought it worthwhile to gun down an unarmed man on a mere suspicion.

Must have been a slow day in Hawkes Harbor.

"You don't remember the shooting? Or what led up to it?"

"I remember waking up after." Jamie rubbed his eyes with the heel of his hand.

That was on the report—prone to severe mood swings, cried easily, bouts of hysteria . . .

"It really hurt," he explained. He looked at the windows. "It's getting dark. Usually, I get a pill about now . . ."

"Of course. In just a moment."

The medical report emphasized the patient's extreme distress at twilight—unless heavily sedated he would not sleep at all at night. And even then, was subject to violent nightmares. And all that had certainly been borne out during these first few weeks at Terrace View.

"That's an interesting scar you have there."

"W-w-what?" Jamie went white. He clamped his left hand over his throat. "There ain't nothin' there."

"I mean the one that looks like a burn? From your shoulder down to your elbow."

Jamie pushed up the short sleeve of his white T-shirt to look, exposing a tattoo of a well-endowed mermaid on his bicep. And to Dr. McDevitt's total surprise, Jamie laughed.

"Hey, that? Shark got me. Got another scar at the same time. From my ass to the back of my knee."

"A shark bit you?"

"Hell no, my arm would be gone if it'd bit me. It was a twelve-foot tiger. No, it just rubbed me good. Maybe it was a lady shark, like Kell said . . . they got hide worse than sandpaper. Took all the skin right off."

"And you find this shark attack humorous?"

"Well, the pirates thought it was funny, that's the important thing. And I thought ol' Kell was going to bust a gut laughing. Said he'd never seen anyone swim so fast."

Dr. McDevitt sighed. There had been no mention in his records of these fantasies. . . .

"The pirates?" he inquired.

"Yeah, we were in the Andamans, smuggling rubies out of Burma. . . ." Seeing the doctor's puzzled look, Jamie added politely, "The Andaman Sea, south of the Bay of Bengal—west of Bangkok? East of Sri Lanka?"

He appeared to be slightly shocked at the doctor's lack of geography. Then he looked at the window. The sunlight had disappeared.

"I think maybe I better get a pill—"

He jumped up and paced.

"Sharks got real dead eyes," he said rapidly. "You ever see one up close? Got dead eyes, you're kinda surprised they're breathin'. . . . I seen dead eyes, though, burnin' like fires of hell. . . . Oh God, it's getting dark . . . don't let it be dark. . . ."

Dr. McDevitt took a deep breath. He was witnessing what he'd only been told of before—Jamie's hysteria at sunset.

"There's nothing to be afraid of in the dark," he soothed.

"The hell there ain't!" Jamie was rapidly losing control. He looked around wildly, as if for an escape. "Bad stuff happens when it's dark. God, what's gonna happen now? Now what? God," he cried, "it's too late. It's dark. It's already dark."

Dr. McDevitt pushed a button on his intercom, called for an orderly and an injection. As rapidly as Jamie's hysteria was escalating, a pill would take too long.

"What bad stuff, Jamie?"

"You know. I can't stop it!" He paced, his eyes wild and empty. "I can't do nothin' about it! I'm too tired." His voice trailed off into a sob. "I'm too tired . . ."

"Jamie," said the doctor, "you're going to need an injection now. I'm going to try not to be late with your medication again."

"Don't hurt me." Jamie gripped the back of his chair. "Please."

Lee advanced with the hypodermic; Jamie offered no resistance.

The orderly left, and Jamie slumped back into his chair.

His eyes gradually dulled as the tranquilizers took effect. His breathing returned to normal.

Something nagged at the doctor's memory. Yes, here it was in the police record—Jamie's deportation from three countries. Suspected of smuggling. Could any of this story be true? He shuffled through the papers, found a worn and well-stamped passport.

"Hey," Jamie said. "That's m-m-mine."

"Of course it is, Jamie. We're just keeping it for you. You can have it back."

"Okay," he muttered. "But don't lose it. I never lost a passport. Kell said I was the only person he knew who never lost a passport. . . . You know, Kell had a U.S. passport, but he wasn't a citizen . . . he was Irish. But he had a couple. Knew where to get good fakes."

"So, Jamie, sometime will you tell me about your shark attack and the Burmese pirates?"

"Yeah. Wish Kell was here, though. He could tell a story. We had drinks on the house every time. . . ." Jamie's voice trailed off drowsily.

Dr. McDevitt called for an orderly, and Jamie left docilely for his room. The doctor made a note. He must always schedule Jamie's sessions in the mornings. It would probably be a while before he was weaned from the strong evening sedation.

Once the young man had gone, the doctor couldn't help glancing at the darkened window. Interesting story, yet how much of what he said was true? The doctor suddenly looked away, wondering what the dark could contain that could terrify a man who had faced Burmese pirates. Who laughed at sharks.

Andaman Sea
MARCH 1964

"Well, Jamie, if you don't hurry and get that engine started, we'll cook."

"I'm working as fast as I can. It's hard to breathe down here. Anyway, you want it done right, don'tchya?"

Jamie came up from the engine room. He was dripping sweat. He was wearing only a pair of cotton drawstring pants, but they were soaked and clinging to him and he seriously considered taking them off, too. It was easily 100 degrees, and a bright sun reflecting off the clear water, the white sand of the beach and cove, added to the heat.

He could use a swim anyway. First, a cigarette.

Jamie sat down at the table under the boat's awning and tapped a cigarette out of the package that lay there.

"Whoever thought this tub was a pleasure boat didn't know what pleasure was," he remarked.

It was a nice little one-cabin cruiser, or had been once. Fifteen years and a lot of rough use had changed it considerably.

"Well now, Jamie, we can be buyin' our own yachts, now, can't we? This tub got us out of Rangoon, and it'll get us to Sri Lanka. That's all that's needed."

Kellen Quinn sat idly in the seat behind the wheel. Other than constantly adding up how much money they'd have waiting for them in Bangkok, there wasn't much else he could do at this point.

Jamie picked up a water jug and took a small, careful swallow. Neither he nor Kell mentioned the fact they were starting to watch the water supply.

"You can fix it, can't you, lad?"

"Yeah. Don't worry." He rubbed at the gold stubble on his chin. It showed up glittering against his tan. His normally dark blond hair was striped gold with sun and salt; his hazel eyes looked almost yellow in his tanned face.

Jamie Sommers was twenty-one years old and he was very, very rich, if he could get to some place where he could spend his money.

"It's a good thing I got those spare plugs." Jamie had insisted on a few parts, once he got a look at the boat that was supposed to get them to Sri Lanka. Parts were harder to find on the black market than rubies, but rubies weren't going to run a boat.

Buy a yacht. Now there was a good idea. Jamie put the dangerous escape from Rangoon out of his mind, letting it wander to how to spend his money.

He'd been thinking along the lines of week-long drunks and very pretty ladies—adding a yacht to that mix was a good idea.

He picked up the worn leather bag that lay on the table. Very carefully—Kell had fits about the pearls getting scratched, but there sure hadn't been time to do any fancy packaging—he slid the contents onto the table.

Pearls. Jade. Rubies.

After two years, it was apparent General NeWin's socialist government wasn't working; most people thought sooner or later it would collapse. Meanwhile, the black market in Burma was a trader's market, medicine, cooking pots, even soap more valuable than pretty stones—

A score waiting to happen for a thinking man like Kellen Quinn, an acting man like Jamie Sommers.

"This one's mine, right?" Jamie held up an 8-carat, teardrop ruby. He liked the rubies the best. Pearls and jade were pale next to rubies. Kell had taught him how to judge jewels—the clarity and color to this one was breathtaking. This one was a keeper. He wasn't going to "translate" it into cash. It made him feel good just to look at it. Yeah, he was keeping this one.

"I told you after you downed that armed guard, whichever one you want."

Kell watched Jamie hold the stone up to the sun. In truth, Kell was the more amenable to this because, as valuable as it was, the ruby was not the rarest of the gems. Several of the very old jade pieces were worth twice as much. And the artifacts—the poor kid showed no interest at all in the artifacts, and they were worth more than the rest together.

Let the kid have his ruby, Kell thought, standing up. He too was shirtless, burned dark by the sun, almost the same dark mahogany as his hair. His Irish blue eyes were startling in his face. Tall, lean, handsome, at first glance Kellen Quinn appeared much closer to forty than fifty. Just a touch of rusty gray in his hair, stubble, a few wry lines around his eyes, belied his youthful appearance.

Kell walked to the back of the boat and leaned over to dip his neckerchief in the sea, wring it slightly, and tie back around his neck.

He glanced out to sea and paused.

"Company," he said.

Jamie slipped the ruby into his pocket but pushed the remaining stones back in the bag.

They were anchored in a large cove of a small island—unmapped, uninhabited, stunningly beautiful, like most of the scattered Andamans. The islands weren't on any shipping routes; and since the political upheaval in Burma they were no place for tourists or anyone else who lived by laws. But they were a very convenient place to rendezvous, to trade cargoes. To hide while you repaired a boat . . .

As Jamie got a closer look at the small ship bearing down on them, he knew it was no pleasure cruiser.

A gunboat. His heart picked up pace.

"If it's military we're dead," Kell said. "Don't do anything foolish, lad."

Jamie glanced at him. He had considered swimming to

shore—it wasn't close, but Jamie was a very good swimmer. He had been checked by the thought that Kell'd never make it. Kell had lived most of his life on the sea and couldn't have swum a horse pond. Besides that, as good as Jamie was, he'd be mowed down before he was halfway there. He knew about machine guns from the navy.

They could see who manned the ship now—not military, but certainly not civilians. Burmese, bare to the waist, loaded with ammo belts, carrying submachine guns and automatic rifles; most wore pistols, too.

Jamie thought briefly of their own pitiful arsenal—Kell's Luger, his own .38—he'd lost the M60 in that scuffle on the docks. Well, that didn't matter now, not against these guys. Anyway, neither he nor Kell was much at gunplay—both would rather use something else: Kell, words; Jamie, fists.

"Pirates," Kell said, and Jamie slipped the ruby out of his pocket and popped it into his mouth.

"You know, I thought I smelled a setup. Cahill was acting a wee bit peculiar."

"If so, we have a hope," Kell said. Jamie loved that about him: Kell always had a hope. "If they know what they're looking for and we make it easy for them to find it, they may leave us alive. After all, a third of the gross national product of Burma these days comes from smuggling; they don't want to scare off trade."

Jamie tried to picture himself and Kell as valuable economic factors . . . then this abstract musing was crowded out by images of the different ways of dying Jamie had heard discussed. . . .

He and Kell stood in plain sight on the back deck as the ship swung alongside of the little cruiser and a few of the machine-gunned thugs boarded.

Kell muttered, "If they think we're hiding something, they'll gut us to search our stomachs, without bothering to kill us first. So no tricks, lad. . . . Welcome, gentlemen." Kell raised his voice in greeting, as if they were long-expected guests.

Jamie had second thoughts about swallowing his ruby; it remained in his mouth like a tasteless mint. There was no way to get it out without calling attention to himself.

He looked at the long, fish-gutting knives that hung from some of the ammo belts. Sucking the ruby helped his dry mouth. The sun and the glare gave him a headache. The sweat seemed to roll down his body in waves.

The pirates barely glanced at Kell and Jamie as they began a thorough search of the boat. Shouting at each other in some foreign babble, keeping any stray items they thought worth the trouble, the pirates systematically tore through the boat.

The leader found the leather bag and was examining the contents, piece by piece. One of the others opened Kell's leather duffel to sort through the artifacts.

The leader walked up to where Jamie and Kell stood sweating in the sun. He held out his hand and growled out something that sounded like "More!"

"Oh, you've got it all, sir, yes, that's the whole kit and caboodle, we'd not be holding out on you, would we, Jamie?"

Kell gave the leader a big smile, and Jamie a friendly slap on the back.

Jamie lurched forward, and in an effort not to swallow, he spit instead. The ruby shot out of Jamie's mouth, across the hot deck, and plopped into the azure water.

And breathing, "Holy shit!" Jamie ran two strides across the boat and dived in after it.

He'd spent weeks pearl diving when they'd been in the French

Polynesians, and the training paid off; in twenty-five feet of clear water, strangely devoid of the usual schools of bright fish, he swam down after the ruby. It was as bright as a drop of blood on the white sands. He fumbled for a minute, it jumped out of his fingers twice, then he swam to the top, the stone clenched tight in his fist.

"Hey," he yelled, shaking back his hair from his eyes. "I got it!"

He grinned at the cheering. Maybe this would buy their lives . . .

"Jamie, look out!" Kell called.

Suddenly he got a feeling that the cheers were not for him.

The pirates were nudging each other, laughing, and pointing at something behind him, running and jostling for a better view, causing the small craft to list dangerously. Jamie looked behind him and saw the slick dark fin bearing down.

He turned and shot toward the boat. Almost immediately he was hit and tossed sideways. He came up swimming fast. In what seemed like a split second, another shove to the butt seemed to almost boost him into the boat, where Kell grabbed him under the arms and hoisted him onto the deck.

Jamie lay huddled, still clenching his fist, his eyes shut tight. He was choking out water, gasping in air.

"K-K-K-Kellen, is everything still on?"

For all he knew, he was missing a limb. He thought he could still feel his arm, his leg, but knew from other's stories that wasn't a reliable indication.

"Yes, Jamie, all your appendages are still attached, including the one you value most." Kell sounded like he was laughing.

Jamie uncurled and got shakily to his feet.

From the back of his right shoulder down to his elbow, the skin was rubbed off; and when the shark had brushed his right leg it'd taken Jamie's pants off, as well as the hide of his buttock and upper thigh.

Jamie stood naked and bleeding and breathing hard with pain. He felt like he'd been skinned and dipped in salt water. He became aware that the pirates were watching him. Speculation? Admiration? He walked up to the leader without a trace of a limp and only a suggestion of a swagger.

"You missed one." He grinned. He held out the ruby and dropped it into the scar-seamed hand.

The pirates burst into guffaws of rowdy laughter, and Jamie knew he'd cheated death twice that day.

"Well, at least they didn't take the whiskey." Kell lay on the deck, studying the stars. He was propped up on his sea bag to take a swig from the bottle.

Jamie lay on his left side, shifting to find a comfortable position, but it was useless. He wasn't going to be able to sit for a week—unless his wounds stopped oozing by tomorrow, he'd sail into Sri Lanka naked.

Jamie took a long pull at the bottle. The pain was as bad as a severe burn, and Kell charitably didn't object to his taking more than his share.

Kell laughed. "By God, Jamie, that was the fastest swimming I've ever seen from a man. We'll have to work up a show—the Jamie Sommers Swimming and Comedy Act. Should be easy from now on—I'm sure you've played your toughest audience."

Jamie chuckled. He could imagine how funny he'd looked, shooting through the water. Kell said he'd been yelling, too, though he didn't remember that.

"Wonder why that shark didn't bite me?"

"Must have been a lady shark. The ladies always like to give you a good rub before they bite, hey, Jamie?"

Jamie grinned but didn't pursue that line of conversation, the ladies being a source of friendly, and sometimes not so friendly, competition between them.

(Besides the occasional competition, their styles were very different. Kell would invest in a long courtship if he had the time; the game was as enjoyable to him as the score. Jamie liked to get right to business, and in Kell's opinion, was too fast to pull out his wallet . . . he was irritated by the fact that Jamie would spend money on what would be easily obtainable for free—

"A handsome young lad like yourself shouldn't have to pay a woman for sex."

"Ain't payin' 'em for sex. Payin' 'em to leave me alone, after."

Jamie was serious, but Kell roared, and often worked that conversation into a story, whether it fit or not.)

"No, Jamie, the shark didn't bite you for the same reason the pirates didn't gut you—your luck was with you today."

Jamie pondered that. In spite of everything, he knew it was true. They had no money, no cargo to trade, no jewels, damn little water, only this rust bucket between them and the schools of sharks, attracted by Jamie's blood, that swam in silent circles around the boat. Once in a while one would bump the boat, giving it a perversely gentle rocking motion.

And yet, his luck was with him. Kell was right about that.

"Well, Jamie, it's been a while since I first saw forty, and I'm getting too old for this line of work. I'm thinking of going to Monte Carlo, finding some rich widows who are susceptible to my charms. If all else fails, I know of one in America who'll be amiable to my persuasions. You coming along, lad?"

A while since Kell had seen forty . . . Jamie had a hard time believing Kell was that old. Probably because he had more energy than anyone Jamie had ever known. The talking alone Kell did would wear Jamie out.

"You're always welcome, you know—you're a scrapper, lad," Kell said. "A born scrapper. Grit. I like that in a man. I admired that about you the first day we met."

Jamie had taken on two guys in a Hawaiian bar, bested them both, mostly because they were drunk and by luck of the draw, he wasn't, and because he was small and very fast, and they were neither.

"Let me buy you a drink, young Jamie," Kell had offered, once the brawl was over.

Jamie took the drink gladly.

"So you're finished with the navy? And what plans do you have now? Well, it's always a good thing to have a plan—but I can see you're a man of action. I'm a man of thought. We could make a team, Jamie."

And then, "So you're familiar with the South China Sea? I have some prospects there. Oil, it'll be big there someday, Jamie. I know a man . . ."

So Kell and Jamie shipped out together. Jamie loved Kell's way with words. He knew how to string them together, make them into weapons, music, dreams. On calm nights, in crew quarters, Kell's brogue would carry through the bunks. Stories, plans, bullshit so pleasant the sailors wished it the truth, forgave him the cons, scams, the cheats he tormented them with—Kell carried visions; they would have forgiven him much worse.

And Jamie, for the first time not lonely, would have forgiven him anything. But had much more sense than to trust him. They'd wandered together for a year, off and on, Kell busy with some business in Malaysia, Jamie working a cargo-liner run from Kota Kinabalu to Brunei, off Borneo, when Kell got wind of this fabulous deal, trading cargoes in Rangoon . . . yes, Burma wasn't the safest of places right now, but it'd set them up for life, he said. . . .

"Yeah," Jamie said now. He searched again for a comfortable position, but he bit back a groan at the pain. "I wouldn't mind a look at the French Riviera." He couldn't help it. "You got a plan after that?"

"We sell insurance in Baltimore."

Kell laughed when Jamie choked on his next gulp of whiskey.

"How much do you think those jewels were worth?" Jamie said, after a long silence.

"Millions, lad. Millions."

Jamie looked up at the stars. He liked the way they changed positions in different parts of the world.

Well, not many men had a chance to hold millions. He lay his head on his arm. He was content with being alive.

Terrace View Asylum, Delaware
JANUARY 1967

"So it's very unusual, for a shark to strike without biting?" Dr. McDevitt asked, in Jamie's next session.

"Yeah. Very. They'll bump you, but always bite. It was a lucky day, all right."

Jamie was quiet. The bright morning light came in the window. Then he said, "I haven't had one in a while."

Riviera

Terrace View Asylum, Delaware
APRIL 1967

It began to bother Dr. McDevitt that Jamie Sommers had no visitors. That was pretty much the norm for Eastern State, especially the wing for the criminally insane, where he'd been kept. But if someone cared enough to foot the expenses at Terrace View, they usually cared enough to visit, if only to see how the money was being spent.

The sad thing about mental patients, the doctor often thought, was as they improved, they became worse; as they became more aware of where they were, why they were there, depression, if it was not present before, set in. If it had been present before, it worsened.

Jamie was no exception. While much less agitated during the day, he was much less animated also. He no longer bothered getting dressed—just put on a robe over his pajamas. He had to be asked to bathe and shave, reminded he had to eat. Some days he couldn't leave his room, could barely leave his bed.

He never had interacted much with the other patients; now, in his sessions with Dr. McDevitt, his hesitant voice seemed rusty from lack of use.

Left in the rec room, he would slowly work jigsaw puzzles by the hour. Many times they would find him on the landing to the third floor, where the window viewed the sea.

But there were some signs of improvement.

He was becoming clearer about his time in Hawkes Harbor— he had worked in an old house, he said, where there were no lights but candles. He had to get firewood . . .

If Dr. McDevitt steered the conversation to the times he roamed the sea with Kell Quinn, he picked up a little; he had no compunction about reciting the most chilling criminal activities as if they were boyish pranks—if Dr. McDevitt understood him correctly, he once confessed to a cold-blooded murder.

That was why Dr. McDevitt tended to believe him when he still insisted he was innocent of any wrongdoing where Katie Roddendem was concerned.

They didn't broach that subject often—it always made Jamie cry.

Perhaps if Jamie had something to jar his memory . . . and a visitor to improve his spirits . . . In one of Jamie's progress reports to Louisa Kahne, the doctor mentioned that if Mr. Hawkes, his former employer, could perhaps take the time . . .

Louisa wrote back that Mr. Hawkes was a very busy man, very pressed for time; maybe someday . . . she herself was acquainted with Jamie, she'd try to get up there soon. . . .

Dr. McDevitt sighed over the letter. He'd see Jamie in a few minutes—he had wanted so much to promise a visitor.

Not that Jamie ever asked for one. Or seemed to notice when other patients had them.

Dr. McDevitt decide to go after Jamie himself, instead of sending a nurse. No doubt he'd be on the third-floor landing.

On the way, the doctor passed another patient of his, eagerly peering out the windows in the lobby. A young math professor, whose foray into a new field of physics—chaos theory—had proven overwhelming for him.

The young man was waiting excitedly for his wife—she'd asked for and received permission to bring their dog.

Dr. McDevitt smiled at his happiness. This one would be able to go home soon, though it was still doubtful if he'd ever be able to resume his studies.

And glancing out the front window with him, he saw that Jamie was sitting on the long lounge sofa on the front porch.

He had permission to go outside, though he never left the porch, always came in at twilight. So far, Jamie had been on two field trips to the small neighboring town, neither a success. On one, he'd become convinced a storekeeper was not speaking English; an unfortunate choice of movies ruined the other.

Jamie was not to see police movies again.

Dr. McDevitt seated himself on the lounge. As good a place to talk as any.

"Hello, Jamie."

"Hey, Doc," Jamie replied, without turning to look at him.

Dr. McDevitt was relieved that Jamie seemed to know who he was—occasionally Jamie called him "Captain." Once, while he sat at the rec-room table to watch Jamie work on a puzzle, Jamie said, "Captain, you know when we'll be sailing? This place is starting to get on my nerves."

Dr. McDevitt felt vaguely flattered to be called "Captain." Perhaps because he couldn't have manned a rowboat. He answered gently, "Not for a while yet, Jamie," and Jamie had sighed. . . .

"So how are you feeling today, Jamie?"

"All right," he answered, staring across the grounds, into the forests. He had deep-set eyes; they always sought the horizon.

A family pulled up in a station wagon, a carload of visitors for someone. Jamie focused on them for a moment and Dr. McDevitt couldn't help it, he said, "Would you like to have a visitor, Jamie?"

Jamie said, "Nobody hardly ever gets visitors in jail. They're scared they won't get back out."

"This isn't a jail, it's a hospital."

Jamie gave him a long look, then sighed. "Anyway, who'd—" Then he grinned. "I take that back."

"Yes?"

"Kell visited me in jail. I have to give him that . . ."

Saint-Tropez, French Riviera
SEPTEMBER 1964

Jamie had no idea what was going to happen to him when the guards took him from the large holding cell he shared with seven

other prisoners—none of them American—to the small room
that held two chairs on either side of a small table.

For all he knew, it was the first stop on the way to being put
up against the wall and shot.

It had been hard enough to keep the American laws
straight—once Jamie started shipping out on foreign vessels, he
paid little attention to laws except for the basics. Some places
frowned harder than others on drugs, some disliked their natives
being beat up by Americans, some were unbelievably picky
about papers. Jamie had both legitimate papers and very good
forgeries, tried to think twice about fights, and unless getting
paid top dollar for smuggling, left drugs alone.

But now, without the excuse of poor papers, no recent fights,
and a long abstinence from drugs for personal use, much less dis-
tribution, here he was.

And here he might stay. For a long, long time.

He sat in the small room, shivering slightly—he'd been running a fever since the gendarmes roughed him up, arresting him.
He shouldn't have tried to run. Easy to say, now.

He didn't expect to see Kell Quinn being ushered in as a visitor. He hadn't seen Kell in months.

And he didn't expect to be so glad he could have burst into
tears.

And so mad he could have slugged him.

But mostly, and for the first time in the twenty-four hours
since the arrest, hopeful.

Kell sat across the table from him.

To break the silence, but especially to keep Kell from saying,
"I told you so," Jamie said. "Got a cigarette?"

Kell took a pack and a matchbook from his blazer pocket
and tossed them.

Jamie lit up and offered the pack back. Kell shook his head.

"Keep them." He paused, knowing almost anything he said would make Jamie angry, but he was angry himself . . . fool kid.

"Well, Jamie, this *is* a mess you've got yourself into. A diplomat's daughter, a count's fiancée, and not out of her teens. You might try keeping your brains where you don't have to unzip your pants to get at them. It's wonderfully convenient."

"Not my fault," Jamie said sullenly.

"Sure it's not, lad. The lady raped you, instead, is that what you're sayin' now?"

Jamie knew it sounded ludicrous. "Yeah, that's about it."

Kell almost got to his feet and left—he wasn't in the mood for nonsense.

But poor Jamie looked so miserable. . . .

"You're needing stitches in that." Kell gestured toward the split on Jamie's cheekbone.

"It don't matter," Jamie said.

"Resisting arrest on top of everything else."

"I panicked," Jamie said. "You know I don't speak French, I didn't know what they wanted. . . ."

But at the sight of the gendarmes coming up the gangplank, Jamie had had a horrible feeling it was something to do with him. And something to do with that rich bitch . . .

"Jamie," Kell said, "surely a fine lad like yourself, in a place like the Riviera, doesn't need to be forcing himself on a girl."

"Didn't force her."

"I saw the police report. Her lip required stitches—bruises all over her body—"

Jamie yanked down the neck of his T-shirt. "See that?"

He pointed to a festering sore on his collarbone. "Bit me clear to the bone."

Kell could see his neck was bruised black-and-blue with bites.

"And my back's clawed raw—if she'd been trying to get away it'd been my face, right?"

Kell thought about it, studying Jamie's face. Jamie was not a good liar, which did not mean he would not lie.

Jamie went on: "Remember Cahill—how he said he liked to hurt them—couldn't get off, he said, unless they were trying to get away—said nothing turned him on like real screams?"

Kell nodded. "Go on."

"Remember what you said about it—it must be like being addicted or something? They even threw him out of that whorehouse in Bangkok. Well, Kellen, you ever know me to hurt a woman? I never have, don't want to, ain't my style. Hell, if I never screw again it's fine with me . . . that sick rich cunt . . ."

"Jamie," Kell said, "they took photographs. Somebody roughed the girl up. Are you saying it wasn't you?"

Jamie slumped in his seat.

"It was me all right," he said, defeated. "But it's not what you think."

Jamie and Kell had had one of their occasional fights in Monte Carlo.

They could get along most of the time. Their flare-ups were usually caused by Kell's natural desire to be the boss—he was older and much wiser, after all—and Jamie's natural desire not to be bossed, because he didn't give a fuck who was older and wiser, after all.

In the very foreign ports, the dangerous ones, they never let a quarrel last.

They were far too dependent on each other, if for no other reason than for the comfort of knowing someone else would care if you died.

Tough, streetwise, good at self-survival in their very different ways, Jamie and Kell together added up to much more than the sum of their parts. They were too aware of this to easily surrender that advantage. What would surprise most people about their relationship was their total lack of trust in each other, which in no way interfered with their sincere affection—Jamie liked to listen while Kell liked to talk; it was perhaps the strongest of their bonds.

Still, in circumstances that gave each confidence in his power to survive on his own, tempers weren't so pliant.

And the French Riviera held no terror for either of them. They could afford the luxury of smoldering resentment.

In Sri Lanka, Kell had collected a small debt owed him and sold the pitiful boat. They had joined a crew on one of the last of the tramp steamers to Bombay, where there was again something owed to Kell Quinn.

Still insisting on working their way, much to Jamie's irritation, since in his opinion Kell could easily afford at least two third-class tickets, they gradually floated west.

"It'll do us good to work, Jamie," Kell said. "Keeps you from getting flabby and soft. And I'll need a large stake on this next caper."

"Easy for you to say," Jamie muttered. "You ain't working half skinned."

Jamie's disposition, which coped easily with sudden violence, wore ugly under constant pain.

And at Monte Carlo, every previous irritation swirled together into a vortex of anger.

Kell went to the casino every night and his moderate stake grew larger.

Jamie promptly lost everything he had.

Kell, ready to move on, told Jamie the only way he would accept him as a partner in his next scam—fleecing rich older ladies—was if Jamie pretended to be his valet.

Kell knew how to act in the playground of the rich; Jamie would be tossed out the first day.

Jamie didn't know how to dress for what occasion, what fork to use at dinner; his ignorance of even everyday manners, not to mention common grammar, would brand him as an impostor within minutes.

Kell might as well bring an orangutan and try to pass him off as a duke, and said so.

Jamie knew most of this made sense—it didn't hurt any less for that fact.

And he wasn't going to be anybody's manservant.

They had ended up swinging on each other—each claimed victory publicly, and privately conceded it.

And even just a few hours later, each missed the other, but not enough to reconcile.

Kell promptly moved into the upper circles, where his easy Irish charm, his quick wit, his careful wardrobe with scrupulous attention to details made everything so natural for him.

Jamie walked the other way and promptly got a job on a private yacht.

He was overqualified for a deckhand.

Though there were many young men looking for yachting jobs on the Riviera, Jamie definitely had an advantage. He could chart, navigate, steer, keep a log, as well as do the usual deckhand duties of bartending and lifeguarding.

The fact that he could also fix almost anything short of major engine problems cinched him the first job he applied for.

He was one of two deckhands—one of seven crew members.

The other deckhand was a Frenchman who spoke little English but knew enough to understood the captain, a tough, bald Brit. He and Jamie shared a crew cabin but little else.

The crew cabin on this boat was the most luxurious quarters Jamie had ever had.

Besides the captain and Jamie's bunkmate, there was a French chef who considered his importance on a par with the captain's and the Italian engineer who had been with the boat since its maiden voyage and referred to the ship as a person.

There were two stewardesses, to housekeep, help wait tables, and do laundry. One was old enough to be Jamie's mother and—typically—mothered him. He was constantly being plied with pastries and cheeses.

And since the food on the last freighter had been nearly inedible, Jamie had gone from slim to gaunt—he was grateful for the pastries and cheeses.

The other stewardess was cute and clean-cut and sleeping with the captain—Jamie steered clear.

Jamie respected the captain, who was tough but fair, always a important factor in what kind of job he did—given a task, he would do a good job. Given an order, he would rebel.

He couldn't take orders from someone he considered a fool; he'd had enough of mindless regimentation in the orphanage, the navy.

Captain Hughes was no fool.

But Captain Hughes had a word of caution for him.

"You ever deal with the rich before?"

"No." Jamie thought bitter thoughts of Kell.

"I'll tell you this, young Sommers—there's law, and there's rich man's law. There's manners, and there's rich man's manners. The sun shines differently for them, the sea rocks special. If you can't live with that, you can't work here.

"Stay away from them, Jamie. They can crumple you like a paper cup and give you as much thought when tossing you overboard. Especially the girls."

It only took a few days to see what the captain meant.

La Petit Trope was a million-dollar motor sailer; she housed twelve guests in six staterooms; there was a bar saloon, an awning to unroll on the upper forward deck for outdoor dining, and a swimming platform in the bottom of aft deck, where the ski boat could dock.

There were teak decks, Lalique wineglasses; the silverware was silver. The sunshine did seem different, more expensive, somehow.

Jamie had learned a lot about sails in the South Pacific; it was his favorite form of boating now, and he loved it when they cut the motors to be wind-borne.

This was a dream job. But there were days when he thought he wasn't being paid enough.

Jamie had always connected riches with old people. Like the benefactors at the orphanage, who seemed to visit only to make sure their names were slapped on a piece of bronze somewhere.

Even at the age of nine, Jamie thought they might be more concerned with the quality of the food served at the orphanage, with the fact that the nuns thought the cure for everything from stammering to cursing to poor reading skills was a good lashing.

Even at nine Jamie thought there might be different approaches to education.

This was his first experience with rich young people.

And Jamie, not at all easily intimated, was intimidated.

They were so sleek, so confident, so sure of who they were. Even the ones who weren't physically beautiful (and there were only a few) had an air of knowing they owned the world.

The girls, especially.

Jamie knew he was attractive to women. He was only five-foot-seven, but he had the muscled shoulders, the slim waist and hips of a swimmer. His hair was a gleaming mane of six different shades of gold, his eyes clear and direct. The women who could resist his slow hot smile fell for his boyish grin. Experienced at sixteen, now twenty-two, with five years at sea behind him, he thought he was expert.

So it was a new sensation—to feel awkward, clumsy, even tongue-tied in the presence of girls. Not that he should be speaking to them anyway, except to ask politely if they would like another drink, another soda.

He had never seen girls like these, all of them tanned, slim, dressed, or rather undressed, in the height of fashion—it was the heyday of the bikini.

And here on the Riviera, some of them didn't bother with the tops. It was the first time Jamie had seen "nice" girls, or at least girls who weren't known whores, parade around in public nearly naked.

And on a ship full of beautiful women there was one who seemed lit by a spotlight.

He couldn't figure out why this one girl was so special—even her beauty was dimmed by her fearless assurance. Her brazenness went beyond bravado—he'd seen tough chicks before.

She owned the world.

Small, she had hair of a dark shiny mahogany red, dark eyes;

she was tanned a deep russet brown. She had a perfect body, breasts as round as small grapefruits—most of the day she only wore an orange bikini bottom, sometimes threw a man's white shirt over it, and somehow made that the perfect uniform for the Riviera.

She spoke so many languages Jamie had a hard time figuring out her nationality, kissed so many men he had a hard time deciding which was the fiancée; altogether, he had a hard time every time he saw her.

He couldn't remember wanting a girl as badly as he wanted this one.

He couldn't even have a good time at a whorehouse; the ones who looked like his passengers were too expensive, the others seemed stale and dull. And not one of them owned the world.

Her name was Selene.

He watched the young rich set skiing and swimming and speedboating, dancing and dining. He served their drinks, did his job, had his fantasies.

He took the first chance he was offered.

The other deckhand, the Frenchman, could swim, but obviously only as an alternative to drowning; Jamie would as soon be in the water as on the boat—no dreams of sharks ever troubled his sleep.

With inward reservations, the captain asked Jamie to keep an eye on the swim platform.

They drank a lot on the swim raft; the pleasant sweet smell of marijuana wafted from that end of the boat.

Jamie gloated when privately asked to add lifeguarding to his duties—Selene was always basking in the sun, like it gave her a deep, sensual pleasure.

He had many thoughts about having her in broad daylight, in the hot sun of the afternoon.

She gleamed in the light like a jewel.

It was late one afternoon, when they were anchored off Saint-Tropez. Jamie was free for a couple of hours; he decided to go for a swim himself if the swim raft was empty.

A hot pallor hung over the ship as it bobbed languidly in the dark blue water. The boat was quiet, it was the hour when most rested for the evening.

Selene was alone on the raft, and she looked up as he paused in the stairwell.

Jamie felt his heart quicken, the immediate throb of desire.

She was stretched out on a large turquoise beach towel, a Tom Collins glass beside her.

Gin and lemon. That was her drink. Jamie made them extra strong for her but could tell no difference in her behavior.

"Need another drink?" Jamie asked. His tongue felt swollen. The air seemed to hang heavy and hot.

She raised her sunglasses and held up her suntan lotion.

"Could you put a little on my back? I can't bear to leave while there is any sun left."

Her English was accented, but he couldn't place it.

Jamie stood motionless. "Sure."

Elation vied with nervousness for only a moment, as he jumped down the stairwell onto the deck.

She rolled onto her stomach. Jamie sat beside her. He could smell lemon juice in her glossy hair, then the coconut scent of the lotion overpowered it.

He had never touched such satiny skin. The lotion slid over it. She was very warm, almost hot, to his touch. She caught her breath, and he smoothed the lotion over her shoulders, down her back, ran a finger gently but firmly down her backbone. He swallowed as she made no move to stop him. He went a short way into the crease of her buttocks. She had a small, heart-shaped butt, just made for gripping.

"Your name is Jamie?" she asked softly.

The sound of his name in her mouth made his heart stop.

"Yes."

"That is very nice, Jamie."

He grew more confident, remembering other female bodies under his hands—

He smoothed the lotion on the back of her legs, thighs, slid his hand under the bikini bottom . . .

The sun hung heavy and hot and motionless in the sky, no air stirred.

Selene sighed and rolled over on her back. She kept her eyes closed under her sunglasses, but her breathing changed. A heavy excitement pushed every thought from Jamie's mind, except for this . . . here . . . now . . .

His hand, still slick with lotion, slid downward—he paused to rub her navel with a gentle finger, exploring . . . mimicking a thrusting motion. Then he slid it between her legs. She moaned, shuddered into climax.

Jamie had tears in his eyes from holding back, his whole body ached with tenseness; he bent over to kiss the lips that had swollen on their own . . . oh God, he couldn't wait much longer.

The stinging slap startled him so much he took almost a minute to realize it came from her.

"And what do you think—I would get personal with a deck-hand? That such a person could kiss me?"

Her voice dripped amused scorn.

"W-w-what?" Of all times for his stammer to reappear. He thought he had never been so hard, so ready . . .

"Go away." She rolled back onto her stomach, but not quickly enough to hide her smirk.

Jamie's face went hot, but he couldn't even grasp at anger, through the intense frustration.

He heard the speedboat coming and stumbled to his feet, to his cabin, while the slap still burned like a brand on his face.

A cold shower didn't help—he had to take care of it the old-fashioned way.

And thinking of her . . .

He had to bartend that night; the guests were all motoring over to a cruise ship for dinner. He was grateful for that.

If he thought he had to wait tables tonight he'd throw himself overboard.

And the way he swam it'd take days to drown.

Selene was a wearing a white Moroccan caftan that clung enough to show she wasn't wearing anything under it.

She was the most beautiful of a set of beautiful girls. And as he went by them with a tray of drinks he heard his name mentioned in a stream of foreign language, the sound of laughter, unmistakable in any language.

He went hot, and later, as she sauntered by him, he felt her hand squeeze his butt.

He had never hated anyone so much. He had never wanted anyone so much. He had never experienced hate and desire at the same time. By the next day it was apparent she was going to continue tormenting him.

He couldn't touch her. But if this went on much longer, he couldn't not touch her.

He would lose control.

He had never hated a woman before, had never even slapped a whore. These violent fantasies were new to him.

But in reality, he dreaded being around her bold smirk. She was always brushing up against him, many times he felt her hand. And he was still so excited by her it was impossible to conceal it.

He knew what she was whispering to her friends, and they laughed at him for it. He knew he should quit before he killed someone.

But he couldn't even imagine what elaborate tale Kellen would make of it, if he quit. He knew he'd meet up with Kell sooner or later; he'd seen him twice on the Riviera, getting into a limo, playing tennis at a hotel where Jamie was picking up guests.

He could just imagine saying, "Yeah, I had a great job till some little rich bitch ran me off."

No girl was going to chase him off this boat.

He stayed and did his job. Got madder, and hotter. It was his first experience with obsession.

And very late one night, when they had cruised back to Saint-Tropez and docked, when the French deckhand was in the town for some kind of family reunion, the captain busy in his cabin aft, and Jamie lay in his bunk, hot-eyed and fantasizing, Selene slipped down the narrow stairs of the hatch and stood next to him.

Wordlessly, he grabbed her wrist and in a second she was pinned under him. He had no thought but vengeance.

She was wearing a short white terry robe; when he yanked it open she was wearing nothing.

He couldn't breathe.

Her eyes glittered in the dark like a cat's.

"I like it rough," she said, breathless.

"You came to the right place," Jamie muttered. He pinned her wrists over her head with one hand, the other grasped a breast viciously.

He kissed her mouth hard, biting to make her lips swell. His knees forced her legs apart.

"You came to the right place."

He entered her immediately, and began acting out his dreams.

And, in the morning, when he lay there, totally exhausted, completely over his obsession, he thought he'd never want to touch a girl again. Jamie thought he was no stranger to perversion, but sex had always been a pleasant activity—if not always accompanied by intense emotional commitment, at least a good-natured desire for mutual fun.

But now—now there would always be the whisper of violence, of hatred . . .

Selene staggered to her feet, picking up her robe. Jamie flinched to see the bruises and welts already rising on that perfect body, the blood on her swollen mouth.

"Thank you very much. Here." She took a few franc notes from her robe pocket and dropped them on the floor next to the bunk.

She tossed back her hair and, moving like a drunk trying to conceal that fact, stepped carefully up the narrow staircase.

Jamie was now feeling the deep scratches down his back, on his buttocks, the bites on his neck—one especially where her teeth had grated on his collarbone and he had barely felt it at the time.

He was ashamed of a night of sex for the first time in his life.

He had been used. No matter what he'd done to her, what sick intense pleasure he'd had, he'd been used.

And when the gendarmes came up the gangplank at noon, all the uneasiness, the shame, the fear crowded thought from his brain and he panicked. . . .

"It wasn't my fault," Jamie said again, but knowing it was hopeless to try to explain it to Kell, and feeling he'd prefer being executed to trying.

Kell sighed. He didn't want to make promises. He changed the subject.

"You look like shit, lad. Is it so bad in here?"

Jamie seemed to have aged years.

"Well, there's an Algerian in here, he's got his eye on me, I can't go to sleep and I didn't sleep the night before," Jamie said. "You got something, Kell?"

He knew Kell was rarely without a shiv in his shoe. And he knew no visitor here was searched too carefully—cigarettes and drugs and money could be bartered with guards.

"Here." Kell took the long-bladed stiletto from his sock and slid it under the table. "Careful, Jamie. If you're caught there'll be nothing I can do."

"Won't get caught." Jamie put the knife in his pocket.

"Can I trouble you for one of my cigarettes?" Kell said.

Jamie tossed him one, and the matches, and bit his lip to keep from begging for help.

He'd deserved a lot of the trouble he'd had in life, but not this. . . .

"Well, Jamie." Kell leaned back, taking a drag on his cigarette. "It must be a fine thing, to be young and handsome and have everyone who sees you, man or woman, dog or cat, looking to rape you."

Jamie stared at Kell, then burst into laughter. There was no hysteria in it at all.

Damn Kell, he was so good. . . .

"Kellen, please." He wiped a tear from his eye, grinning at his old partner. "Get me outta here. Please. I'll do what you say from now on. I promise, I swear my solemn oath . . . please. You always say you have something on at least one official in every port. . . ."

"Ah, Jamie, I have leverage on three here, and I still may not . . . it'll mean calling in valuable chips, lad, remember . . . and money up front as well . . . you'll owe me, Jamie. . . .

"Well, I'll see what I can do. . . . You've a rare smile, Jamie. You should use it more often."

Train to Swiss border
SEPTEMBER 1964

"The girl has an evil reputation, Jamie. You weren't the first she's put in jail. It helped considerably."

Jamie looked out the window, took another pull on his beer. The new stitches in his cheek throbbed. His arm ached, too. The doctor had insisted on an antibiotic when he saw the festering bite—nastier than dog bites, he scolded, he must be careful. "Yeah, sure," Jamie'd said. "I won't let anyone bite me again." Already it was receding like a bad dream. He didn't want to talk about it.

"You're looking better, lad, rested. Did your amorous suitor give up his pursuit? Or perhaps you succumbed to his charms?"

"He's dead," Jamie said. "Tripped and fell on a shiv. It was real peaceful in there, after. Everybody was afraid they'd trip and fall on a shiv. Except me. I don't trip easy."

He met Kell's eyes.

"Well, I'm glad you've rested."

After a silent hour, Jamie asked for the first time, "Where we going?"

"Switzerland. I need to visit my bank."

"You make some money?"

"Some, not as much as I'd hoped—the lady's children got wind of our romance. Just as well. I don't believe I'm quite ready for marriage, after all. Not yet."

Kell paused. "And from there we're going to Liverpool. There's a ship with a special cargo . . . we'll visit my homeland before going on. . . ."

"Liverpool? Aw, man, I hate that place, you know that—"

"Well, Jamie, I did think your eternal gratitude would last longer than an hour."

Jamie stammered lamely, "Uh, it's just so c-c-cold . . . I don't mind Liverpool, Kell, honest."

"I must do my patriotic duty, Jamie, a chore for God and country. Then a trip to Boston . . . I have some friends in Boston who could use a little help. . . ."

Jamie had never understood Kell's explanation of Ireland's "troubles" or his role in it, and didn't care to.

"We ever going anywhere fun?"

"Perhaps Jamaica, or New Orleans, for a holiday, once we get things done—

"Havana," Kell said. "It's too bad you missed Havana in its heyday, Jamie. The women there are just your type."

"Not rich," Jamie said. "That's my type."

"Only in good nature, Jamie."

Jamie leaned back against the seat. It was good to be without tension, to sit and relax and listen to Kell's voice.

The first thing he was going to do in Switzerland was get shit-faced, falling-in-the-gutter drunk. He needed that.

Kell was eloquent on the charms of Cuba.

Jamie dozed, dreaming of the girls.

Terrace View Asylum, Delaware
APRIL 1967

Jamie and Dr. McDevitt sat on the porch watching the math professor play with his dog.

He threw sticks, and the dog would fetch, jumping and leaping, begging for another toss.

"You ever have a dog, Jamie?"

"No. There was a monkey . . . on a freighter out of Singapore . . . It did tricks."

Jamie's speech was halting, slow, the depression so obvious Dr. McDevitt made a note to try a new medication. He glanced at the long belt on Jamie's robe, and made another note.

According to his records, Jamie had withdrawn so completely at Eastern State that they'd used shock therapy. Dr. McDevitt ordered it only for the worst cases, and never if the patient was amnesiac.

Jamie swallowed, blinking back tears.

"I think Grenville forgot about me," he said.

Dr. McDevitt hid his excitement. This was the first time Jamie had shown any memory of the man who was paying the bills here at Terrace View. Grenville Hawkes.

What had triggered it?

"Why do you say that, Jamie?"

"Well, he shoulda come to get me by now."

Jamie watched the golden lab race after the stick, bring it back proudly to his master. Sometimes the man would stop to talk to his wife; the dog sat eagerly waiting.

"You think he forgot?"

"I don't know, Jamie."

"I used to work for Grenville," Jamie said. "At Hawkes Hall."

Louisa Kahne

Terrace View Asylum, Delaware
MAY 1967

After improving for a few weeks, Jamie suddenly relapsed into a quiet stupor. Dr. McDevitt was not unduly worried; he had seen similar behavior before. Often it was just exhaustion from beginning human interaction again.

Jamie usually responded if spoken to; he was far from catatonic. He was still brought to Dr. McDevitt's office three times a week. But if he showed no inclination for talking, even for answering yes or no, Dr. McDevitt did not try to force the issue.

Nothing irritated him more than hearing someone shout questions at a patient, as if he were deaf instead of mad.

This morning Jamie did not even nod hello but sat staring at Dr. McDevitt's desk or, more precisely, at the model ship in a bottle that ornamented it.

Dr. McDevitt said, "Good morning, Jamie," but could see that further inquiry would be useless. The doctor glanced again through Jamie's files.

Jamie had been due for release from Eastern State just before he was transferred here. Not because of any miraculous recovery, but simply because the kidnapping charges had been dropped. Lack of evidence . . . the girl involved too confused to testify—

If Louisa Kahne had not intervened, Jamie very likely would have been transported to the state line and dumped there. It was not unheard of. . . .

It was an act of kindness, generosity, from Jamie's employer, Grenville Hawkes, of course, but:

"Where does Louisa Kahne fit into this?" the doctor wondered aloud.

Jamie raised his head and looked directly at him.

"Dr. Kahne better get out of Hawkes Harbor. She wants to help it, but she can't."

The doctor stared, dumbfounded, then hastily scribbled down those two sentences.

"Why do you say that, Jamie?"

But Jamie Sommers was gone again, perhaps to sea in a masted ship. . . .

Dr. McDevitt looked at the note. *Dr. Kahne?* Surely Louisa wasn't trying to pass herself off as a physician. She had left med school without the degree. Then he remembered her degrees:

history, anthropology, specializing in myth and folklore. Of course, technically she could use the title, but still . . .

What was it she couldn't help? Jamie had phrased it so oddly, as if . . . Yes, the way he said "it." As if "it" were a title, or as if "It" was a name.

Hawkes Hall, Hawkes Harbor, Delaware
JULY 1965

Even from across the great hall, Louisa Kahne felt rather than saw the young man tremble.

"Did you accomplish what I asked?" Grenville asked. He paced the great room with his impatient stride, curiously stealthy for a man of his height and weight.

"N-n-no. I, I c-can't do it."

"Go to your quarters. In a moment I will join you and we'll discuss what you can and cannot do."

Louisa saw Jamie Sommers flinch but leave the room with robotlike resolve.

"Dr. Kahne," Grenville said, "I believe volume six contains some mention of what we were looking for. You will excuse me for a moment."

Louisa met his eyes. She hastily looked down at the scattered piles of books and documents and began a fumbling search. Her hands were shaking.

Within a few minutes of Grenville's departure, she heard a low, despairing wail from the back of the hall. Louisa swallowed. Some of her brash self-confidence ebbed, for the first time since she began this . . . project.

Grenville returned, and as if there had been no interruption, seated himself opposite Louisa across the large rough-hewn table.

She slid an old, leather-bound ledger before him.

"Is this what you were speaking of?" she said coolly. "I'm quite certain this is what you meant."

Several hours later Grenville started to open the front door for her, but Louisa stood resolutely in the hallway. She had made up her mind.

"I want to see Jamie before I go."

"Jamie seemed indisposed. He's not receiving visitors."

"There are questions I feel he can answer."

"Not this evening . . ."

She ignored the malevolent look he gave her and went through the large hallway that led to the back of this . . . house? Fort? Castle? Modeled after a hunting lodge in England, he had told her. Never intended to be the main residence . . .

The last door in the hallway was shut; she pushed it open without knocking.

She had a quick impression of a spare, bare, L-shaped room, then saw Jamie sitting on the edge of a narrow bed, rocking back and forth.

He gave a violent start as she opened the door—then calmly said, "Hello, Dr. Kahne," as if she showed up in his room every evening.

She had noticed this about him before. In spite of his nervous edge, the way any unexpected happening made him jump, he still had the air of a man who had experienced the biggest surprise life could hand him, never again could he feel awe.

In a way, he very much resembled the new kind of patient

they were starting to get at Terrace View—the young veterans of the war.

And it's so cold in here, she thought, her own teeth chattering, no wonder he's shivering . . . far too cold for summer.

He moved away as she reached out to touch him.

"I'm okay," he said politely. "I appreciate it, but I'm okay."

He'd been crying.

"Are you sure?"

"Yeah. Just a little dizzy. Weak. It'll pass." Jamie always spoke politely, but hesitant, as if he wasn't quite sure how. He gingerly touched his turtleneck sweater on the right side of his throat.

"This ain't that bad. Anyway, I heal up real fast. It's part of . . . being like this."

"Here." Louisa opened her purse. She took a bottle of capsules, shook two into her hand. "Stronger than aspirin."

"No, thank you. He wouldn't like it."

"What do you mean?" Louisa saw, with queasy pity, a light bloodstain seeping through the sweater.

Jamie thought he couldn't be much clearer, but explained, "He don't want me drinkin', smokin', taking pills. Messes up my blood. I tried to take aspirin before, couldn't get 'em into my mouth."

He was lucky to get to eat and sleep, he thought. Grenville could and had stopped that for a time, too.

"Could have been worse," Jamie said.

"Surely, he doesn't beat you."

Jamie stared at the floor and said nothing. This woman was so naive. . . . Like It needed to do that. . . .

"So. You going to cure It?" Jamie still thought of Grenville as "It."

"Perhaps 'cure' is an incorrect word in this case. I don't see the affliction as an illness. I would like to be of help, however."

"He told me it wouldn't make any difference to me. I'd still be . . ."

Fucked up, Jamie stopped himself from saying. "Like this."

Powerless. Helpless. In Its power. No will of his own.

"Don't ya want to be cured?" he'd asked It, when It had been debating Louisa's offer of help.

"It will make no difference to you. Only death will set you free," It had replied.

Well, Jamie had known that already. Was trying to do the best with what he had.

Louisa looked a little conscience stricken. "Honestly, I haven't thought of the possible effect on the victims."

"Victim," Jamie corrected. "I'm the only one—alive."

Louisa tried to gather her much-valued self-possession. I am a researcher, an investigator, she thought, this is the case of a lifetime, I will be able to prove the link between the psychic and reality, the actual existence of two planes, I cannot, I will not become personally involved. I will take advantage of this opportunity calmly. . . .

"What's it like?" she asked.

Jamie had no words for her, but he thought, You just keep on the way you're going, lady, you'll find out soon enough.

She had no idea what she was messing with. You could tell she thought she was pretty damn clever; but Grenville Hawkes thought she was a fool. Jamie had to agree. But still, she had a lot of guts.

"You were bitten?"

Jamie's skin crawled at the image her words evoked.

Taken. Used. Branded. Owned.

"How many times?"

"Four or five . . ."

Jamie stared off into space. He was going crazy.

He could feel it. Today, he was refinishing a windowsill, and looked at his watch to see he was missing three hours. His mind had just left; he had no idea where it'd gone.

Maybe next time it wouldn't come back.

He'd looked out the window to see the setting sun, barely had time to get outside before he puked.

He started shaking at sundown, these days.

He was so tired. He was so tired.

And this week, buying varnish and sandpaper and candles at the hardware store, Jamie lost his ability to understand language—all he could hear was gibberish, he had no idea how to speak.

He'd had to run out and leave all the stuff there and just missed being punished for it.

"But he can't really use it now. It just . . . keeps me in line."

"He can no longer use your blood?"

"He has to go get fresh. Mine is too much like his now."

That's why sunlight seared his eyes these days. He was always cold. The smell from Vinnie's Spaghetti House made him gag. He had to avert his eyes to pass the chapel. He had to stay awake in daytime, to guard it, run the errands, but found it very hard to sleep at night.

Jamie wondered how long it'd take Grenville to kill him, once It realized he was crazy.

From the beginning, It had threatened him with the most horrible death possible, even given him a small sample in the effort to break his will—

Jamie hummed as he rocked, Dr. Kahne forgotten. The mon-

ster had reached from the coffin, taken the cur by the throat—
broken him, trained him by cuff and by kick—found him surprisingly useful, but expendable—

Jamie's feelings were much more complex.

He saw the evil, the cruel caprice, the almost random violence. It controlled his behavior now, sometimes even his
thoughts.

He was totally dependent on this being who thought no
more of him than of a fly—his existence was so tied to It he
couldn't imagine freedom.

Only death.

His greatest fear was Its anger, his only pleasure Its rare praise.
He could no more rebel against It than raise his hand to God.

Jamie wanted to know why. An event of such magnitude . . .
why him?

And he wanted desperately to matter to It. As long It needed
him, he could live.

So maybe that was why he found himself thinking "we,"
"us," "our."

In this together.

We   Us   Our

Like It was his old buddy, his old pal.

His old pal.

His old pal.

His old pal.

Jamie's mind played the phrase like a broken record, yet the image it tried to conjure failed to appear.

His mind was such a spook house these days, he never knew
what screaming fright would leap out to send him reeling.

Grenville was getting worse—each time he tried and failed to control his . . . need, his temper worsened.

Its family here in Hawkes Harbor still remained aloof.

And Grenville was becoming paranoid, afraid the deputy sheriff was suspicious.

You can't just kill Mitch Morgan, Jamie told It. People would notice if he disappeared. They'd turn the town upside down, looking for the deputy. . . .

Not like—

Not like—

Jamie's mind balked like a weary beast of burden. Refused to go that road.

And the little kids, Ricky Hawkes, Trisha Pivens—Ricky knew something was wrong, evil, Trisha far too curious and brave for her own good.

Surely Grenville wouldn't hurt kids, Jamie said, little kids, not twelve years old. . . . He'd be sorry, after. . . .

Sometimes Jamie thought It listened to him. . . .

Jamie rocked, remembering the good times he and Ricky and Trisha had had, sitting on the upper outside landing of the boardinghouse, looking across the bay at Hawkes Island, talking of legends . . . the island was riddled with caves, they told him, and the caves rumored full of pirate loot. . . .

He never, ever, meant to hurt those kids. . . .

Jamie sobbed, then wiped his face with his hand.

He couldn't stop It.

He had to stop It.

But if there was a cure . . .

"It will be a great step for our understanding of the human

pysche, of mankind's history and power of mind, if I succeed in helping here." Her voice broke into his thoughts.

Jamie stopped rocking, his mind jerked back into the present. He looked at her. And realized the truth.

Step for human psyche, hell, he thought.

He'd seen that look on a woman's face before. That goofy, besotted look.

Going to help him. Going to change him. Going to give him a reason to reform.

Jamie had been through that with a couple of women himself.

All It needed was the love of the right woman, this walking dead thing.

Yeah, Dr. Kahne was going to make ol' Grenville settle down and stop killing people. Quit all this lusting for blood.

No use trying to talk sense to her. When women got like that, doctor or shop clerk, you could get right in their face and yell, "Hey, look, I'm just after a quick dip in the ol' panties, then I'm outta here." And they'd twist it into words of love.

Except Grenville had no interest in Dr. Kahne's panties at all—but was fascinated by the possibility of reversion. . . . Maybe It'd be more human then, Jamie thought, not so deadly— sometimes Jamie thought It might want to be more human.

Sometimes he was almost sorry for It. It'd been so long in that cave—all It had to think about was the life It'd missed, the love It'd lost—no wonder It seemed insane sometimes, locked up like that, so long—once It had even told him, "I was not always such a monster. The human Grenville Hawkes was very different, Jamie."

Jamie wondered what It would be like as a human. . . . He had a feeling, though, one way or another, Jamie Sommers wouldn't be around to find out. He was at the top of a tall mast, and his grip was slipping. Once in a while he'd drop a few inches, then catch himself—but there was a long free fall coming. He could feel it.

"It's lonely," Jamie said suddenly.

"What do you mean?

"It's—He's lonely. Scared. He has to hide so much. His family don't seem to care. He thought at first he could control everything, but he can't. He can't even control himself."

Jamie thought if she wanted It cured, maybe she would help It when he was gone. Strange, how that instinct to protect It, guard It was so deeply imbedded now . . . "And he hates himself, hates the way he is. He says he don't but—"

Sometimes Jamie thought this was too much for anything to bear, this kind of loneliness. . . .

They both started as the wind shook the outside shutters like a fierce beast demanding entry.

"He hates me, too," Jamie said.

His eyes were feverish, and Louisa reached out to feel his head.

She was frightened by how violently he flinched.

"Why would he hate you?"

"I turned him loose."

Louisa tried to think of words of comfort. Dear God, what comfort was there, in a life like this? Once more she shivered. They both fell silent.

"It's after Katie."

Louisa was confused, uncertain of his whisper.

"Jamie is very fond of Katie Roddendem." Grenville stood in the doorway.

Jamie's eyes closed and for a moment Louisa Kahne thought he would faint.

"I must insist on your departure, Dr. Kahne. I have plans for this evening and my servant needs his rest."

Jamie resumed his rocking, staring straight ahead, humming, and Dr. Kahne looked at him, helpless.

Now she saw the deep lines of despair, the dark hollows under his eyes, the nervous tic in a facial muscle.

This boy is going mad, she thought suddenly.

"Let him go!" she cried. "For God's sake, let him leave!"

"Of course," said Grenville. "Jamie, would you like to leave?"

"No," Jamie said.

"See, Dr. Kahne? It's his own choice, entirely. It's of his own free will."

Kellen Quinn

"You have a lot of nightmares, Jamie," Dr. McDevitt said. Jamie was progressing almost daily now, only an occasional setback.

"Yes."

"Do you ever remember any of them?"

I remember the good dream, Jamie thought, but then, the doctor hadn't asked about the good dream, and Jamie wouldn't have told him anyway—but he remembered *it* quite well.

I'll never forget you Jamie—

In a way it was worse than the nightmares; it hurt so much to wake from, to know it was a dream.

But then there was always the hope of having it again.

Jamie didn't want to think about the bad ones. The ones that left him screaming; sometimes he had to be sedated, and sometimes that got rough.

Probably half of them are about being in a hospital, Jamie thought.

Dr. McDevitt noticed his faint smile but didn't question further.

"Yeah," Jamie said, frowning slightly now in concentration, rubbing his jaw. "I can remember one, I have it a lot. It's always the same. It's bad, it bothers me a lot, because I keep thinking about it."

Jamie sighed. "But it's probably not as bad as the others."

"Why would you say that?"

"Well, because I can remember it."

The doctor received a look he often got from patients, the one that said, "I'm crazy, not stupid."

"What happens in this dream?"

"Well, me and Kell are on this boat, it's a small boat—not a ship—like the one we had in the Andamans, and we're in a storm, a North Atlantic storm, but I can't figure out why the hell we'd be in the North Atlantic in a boat that small. . . . I don't much like the North Atlantic, it ain't my favorite sea."

Jamie stared off.

"Me and Kell ran that transatlantic route four times with those goddamn guns. He kept telling me we were going to New Orleans, and we kept taking guns to Ireland."

"In your dream?"

"No. No. We really were smuggling guns—out of Boston, Gloucester, really—but we always got paid in Boston—the Irish mob was sending guns to the IRA and Kell got gung-ho into it."

"I've understood Northern Ireland has been quite peaceful in the last few years."

"Yeah, but it ain't gonna last much longer, they're getting organized—I never paid too much attention, really. It was just a job.

"I hated it. Those Irish gangsters scared the shit outta me, anyway, the way they could be all smiling and friendly one minute and blow your head off the next—I saw one—

"Anyway, Kell got just like them when he was around them, made me nervous.

"'One more run, Jamie,' he kept saying. 'Just one more. Then it's off to a fun kind of place—maybe New Orleans.'"

Jamie paused. "The money was good, though. The money was real good. And I finally did get to New Orleans."

"In your dream, you're in the North Atlantic in a small boat with Kell."

The doctor looked at his notes.

"Oh yeah, the dream . . . and it's cold, real cold, that ocean always seems cold to me—some places on it really give me the creeps—and we're in this mother of a storm, thirty-foot waves, the ocean just dropping out from under us, the sea and the rain getting all mixed up together in the wind, like it gets sometimes— makes you feel like you're upside down or something—everything is just wet gray haze and the wind howling like a wild thing. . . .

"I'm behind the wheel, trying to keep us headed, but I can't believe we're going to make it, me and Kell yelling at each other, and a wave hits and Kell's gone, just washed out to sea.

"I'm yelling, 'Kell! Kellen!' because I think he's still close somewhere, I'm even thinking maybe I should try to get out and save him—I can swim in pretty rough water, have lots of time, but then, I hear him yelling, 'Go on, Jamie' or 'Keep going, Jamie!' something like that, and then he yells 'Steer by—' "

Jamie stopped. He wiped the tears from his face, and for a minute didn't speak.

"I never hear what it is I'm supposed to steer by," he said. "There's no instruments, no stars, a boat like that, a storm that big—there's nothing.

"But Kell's telling me to go on. . . ."

Dr. McDevitt still looked down at his notes. He'd been in practice many years; Jamie had no idea how disturbed he was by the dream.

They both sat silent for many minutes.

"Sometimes I wonder whatever happened to ol' Kell after he got run outta Hawkes Harbor."

"Perhaps you'll see him again sometime."

"I don't think so," Jamie said. "It's just a feeling I got."

North Atlantic
NOVEMBER 1964

"Your friend, Quinn, he's really funny," Steve Malloy commented.

"Yeah," Jamie said, proud that on a ship full of yarn spinners and bullshitters, Kell still stood out.

"That story he tells, about you and the shark and the pirates—is that true?"

"Mostly," Jamie answered. Kell had a couple of different versions of it by now. One gave you nightmares, one made you wet your pants laughing.

"How about the one where you get raped by a royal princess?"

Jamie clenched his jaw. Goddamn Kell, I'll kick his butt. . . . "He don't tell that one around me."

Steve quickly changed the subject. He'd seen Jamie in a fight. He didn't know it was almost routine for Jamie, a fight on every ship. Because he was small, someone usually thought he could be bullied—he'd correct that misconception and everything would be peaceful again.

"You're lucky you've got your military over with. You see any action?"

"I was in the South China Sea, you had to be battle-ready, but no, nothing you could call action. There's always a bunch of guns there, though. Every goddamn country in the world wants to claim that sea. There's all kinds of gunships strutting up and down, playin' 'who's got the biggest dick.' Lots of trade routes. Me and Kell went back there after. Same ol' stuff going on."

Jamie dealt another hand of cards. He and Steve had to be the worst card players on this ship, so they usually played each other and kept a paper score. Even in the mess room it was bitterly cold, and Jamie had his navy watch wool cap pulled down tight on his head and folded back over his ears.

Jamie usually kept to himself on a ship. It was easier that way. Besides, he had lived most of his life with a complete lack of physical privacy—the orphanage, the navy, close crew quarters; he tended to overcompensate with intense personal privacy. He had no need to get close to anyone. The usual banter of insults and brags that passed for conversation on a ship was fine with him.

Still, there was usually one guy or another you hung around with more than the rest, eating, playing cards. He wasn't seeing much of Kell this trip. Kell had grown up with some of the crewmen; they were full of old stories and in-jokes. One minute they'd sing songs so sad you'd want to throw yourself overboard, and then they'd dance a damn jig the next.

Steve Malloy, who was the closest to his own age, seemed determined to be his friend. It was okay with Jamie. Steve was a nice guy. This was his first time out as a deckhand. His father had told him to make sure he liked it before joining the merchant marines.

"You like the navy?" Steve asked.

"Learned a lot, but I got sick of taking orders. You get a bad officer, it's hell. Regulation haircut, regulation shoes, felt like people were watching to make sure you took a regulation piss. Soon as I got out of there I went to the South Pacific. Didn't cut my hair for a year, went barefoot, and pissed anywhere I damn pleased. You ever been to the South Pacific?"

"No."

"You'd like it. The girls are real friendly. *Real* friendly. Great place to surf. Kell got bored there, but I liked it. Gonna go back sometime, restore a little ketch, do some trading island to island." Jamie was having doubts about he and Kell ever scoring big enough to get a yacht, and anyway, you'd probably have to hang around with rich people, and Jamie had had enough of those bastards.

"I wouldn't mind going back to the South China Sea, either. I had a job on a cargo liner there for almost a year. Best job I ever had—best captain. Captain Harvard. He was Dutch, most of us couldn't say his name—we called him Captain Harvard. Most of the crew was Kiwis. Harvard said sea captains went back in his family four hundred years, and I believe it. He sure knew what he was doing. It was a hell of a fun route—if you could load it, Harvard would carry it. And room for about eight passengers, too. You got a lot of odd ducks in that part of the world."

"Why'd you quit?"

"The ship caught fire and sank. We all got off, thanks to the captain."

Jamie wished he could tell the ship's burning like Kell could. Sometimes Jamie forgot Kell hadn't been there.

"We were waitin' around in Borneo, to see if Harvard was getting another ship, when Kell shows up with his bright idea about smuggling jewels outta Burma. You heard how that turned out. . . . They still got cannibals in Borneo, you know that?"

Sometimes Jamie thought about going back, seeing if he could sign back on with Harvard. There hadn't been a man on-board who didn't trust that guy with his life, and some had crewed the ship for fifteen years . . . but there was always a list of people wanting those jobs. The only reason Jamie got on in the first place was that Kell knew someone. . . .

"You're shittin' me, man." Steve wasn't hard to please.

Jamie liked that about Steve—for once Jamie got to be the talker. And he didn't have to make anything up, just told the truth. Steve hadn't been around too much.

"I'm going to get a little powerboat for the weekends. Tracy likes boats."

Tracy was Steve's girlfriend. He was planning on getting married. Between the powerboat and the marriage idea, Jamie decided Steve was about the most boring person he'd ever come across, even if he was a nice guy.

"Oh man"—Steve voiced his most common worry—"I hope I don't get drafted. It just don't seem fair, something can swoop down and change your life like that."

"Aw, join the navy—at least you know you don't get sea-sick. You'd be surprised how many guys have a real problem with that. I heard they might get the *New Jersey* outta mothballs. I could even stand to take a few orders, if I got a chance to be on a battleship."

"You ain't hearing me, man. I don't want to be in the navy, I don't want to be at sea. I'm quitting after this voyage. Glad I listened to Dad, no way I could do this the rest of my life."

"Why?"

"I get homesick. Don't you ever get homesick?"

"Never had a home to get sick for. Grew up in an orphanage."

In a way, Jamie thought, the ocean was like home to him. If he was away from it for very long, he missed it. And no matter where in the world he was, he felt at home when he saw the sea. Homesick . . .

A grim smile passed across Jamie's face.

"That place burned down while I was in high school. Wish the fuckin' nu—"

"Now, Jamie."

Kell came in with his good pal First Officer Alan Gregory. "That's no language to use about nuns. It's bad luck on any ship, and I won't hear it, besides."

Most of the crew would soon be drifting in. The mess room was the evening gathering place.

"Aw, Kell, you don't believe in that cr—stuff, do you?" Jamie had often seen Kell cross himself in dangerous situations. He thought it was habit or superstition or something. Even for a sea-faring man, Kell was very superstitious. Jamie himself took note of omens—you had to, if you wanted to live at sea—but that was about as far as it went with him.

"It's mother's milk to some of us, lad," said Gregory. The captain was half drunk, half nuts; First Mate Gregory ran things on the ship. Kell thought he was very clever. He set Jamie's teeth on edge.

"Hasn't stopped Kell from much," Jamie pointed out.

"Yes," Kell said. "No doubt I'll spend a good long while in purgatory. If I go first, Jamie, light a candle for me, say a prayer for my soul."

He laughed and went to get a cup of coffee.

Jamie said nothing. He hadn't said a sincere prayer since he was eight years old; it was unlikely he'd start now, even for Kell's soul.

Gregory paused for a minute, studying Jamie. He had cold eyes, Jamie thought. The color of guns.

"I see who 'tis you're remindin' me of now—it's the coloring that fooled me. Young Timothy, Kell's brother."

Jamie said nothing.

"He was a quiet little hothead, too."

When Gregory was not quite out of hearing, Jamie remarked, "He's so full of shit."

Steve looked nervously after Gregory.

"God, be careful, Jamie. You don't want to piss that guy off."

"He can kiss my ass," Jamie said.

"I heard stories."

In spite of the cold, Jamie began to sweat. He wiped his hands on his sweater. What did Steve suspect?

"Stories like what?"

"Like he's killed people, back in Ireland, and one on the docks in Boston and was too smart to get caught."

"Yeah. Maybe so," Jamie said. He relaxed a little. Obviously Steve didn't suspect about the guns. And he was really naive if he thought Gregory was the only man aboard who'd killed someone. . . . Jamie had never seen such cold-eyed killers.

"You don't believe in God?" Steve asked.

"No," Jamie said. "Do you?"

"Well, I'm not a Catholic like a lot of these guys, but I believe in God."

"Why?"

"I don't know, I just do."

"That is so dumb. When you're dead, you're dead."

"I don't think so, Jamie."

"Look," Jamie said, "all I ever heard at the orphanage was 'You're going to hell, Jamie,' 'God loves you, Jamie.' Okay—I'll go to hell and if God loves me He can come and get me. Maybe I'll believe something then."

More men were coming in, a poker game starting, someone trying the radio. Everyone was griping about the cold.

"Well, boys," Kell said, "it's cold—but I've been colder. Almost froze to death, in fact."

The men paused in their griping, coffee drinking—even the poker game slowed. They recognized a story coming. Kell rarely told one, they were always anxious for more. Jamie grinned. He knew this one.

"Yes, faced death in the snow in Switzerland with a good friend of mine, it's amazing what you can find out about a man in a time like that. And I'm speaking of your own first mate, Greg."

Greg glanced up and nodded. Jamie was surprised. He didn't know the guy in the story was Gregory.

"It was during the war, Greg and I had some business in a little village in Switzerland, never mind what now. It was dangerous, but we were harebrained young scamps in those days— exchanging information, finding out things, letting things be found out—that sort of thing."

You could see Kell being a harebrained young scamp, but the men were glancing sideways at Greg. He wasn't known for a sense of humor. Except for a tight little circle of pals, most of the crew was afraid of him; he was hated by a few.

"Anyway, we concluded business, and a few pleasures, and started back to Zurich in our jeep. We'd stocked up on a few essentials, mostly wines and cigarettes, for friends, of course. It was cold and snowy and night but we were already late so we set out anyway. We knew we were in trouble, hoped to buy a little favor—leaving relative luxury, going back to relative hell. Didn't work though. They shipped us off to Africa soon after . . . but that's a different story.

"We were testing the wine, making sure it was good enough for our friends, and became somewhat befuddled, took the wrong road, and ended up in the mountains. Of course we ran out of petrol and blamed each other. But I remember distinctly, Greg, that was your job."

Gregory said, "No it wasn't," in his oddly toneless voice.

"Well, we remember it differently, then. . . . We soon realized cursing each other wouldn't save our butts—in fact we sobered up enough to realize we might die. Nothing will sober you up like cold.

"Was it you or me, Greg, who remembered passing a shack of a cabin? Might have known you'd say that. But you were as muddled as I was, no use pretending for the sake of the crew."

Greg's thin-lipped mouth twisted into his weird little half smile that always made Jamie think of sharks.

"So we salvaged what we could from the jeep and started trudging back. It was the kind of cold that ate your bones from the inside out, felt like a knife in your lungs. The wind lashed tears from your eyes and then froze them into icebergs, and the shivering sapped all your strength, there was none left to walk. You wanted just to curl up and get it over with. Greg kept saying his dick was froze—I lost a couple of toes, myself.

"I tell you, boys, the sight of that cabin was as welcome as if it had been a home for wayward girls. There was a stove, a bed, a little wood, and more outside—it was like we'd stumbled into heaven. Soon had a fire going, the mattress thrown down next to the stove. Neither of us had slept for days; we were tired to say the least.

"Well, me and Greg grew up together, it wasn't like snuggling with a stranger. Pretty soon we were huddled up, just getting ready to doze off, and Greg says, 'Kell, would you care to hold my wiener?' "

The room went silent.

"Well, this startled me, to say the least, but we were both tired and somewhat muddled, since we'd celebrated our near escape with another bottle of wine, so I say, 'No thanks, Greg, the only wiener I care to hold is my own, and it's so cold I couldn't find it with a flashlight.' "

Someone choked on a laugh but quickly recovered.

"Well, we're quiet and nodding off and Greg says, 'I wish you'd hold my wiener, Kell, it's froze.'

"I was thinking all kinds of things by then—but I didn't want to run out in the snow. I really didn't even want Greg to move, he was as warm as a horse blanket—I'll overlook the odor comparisons. I'm thinking, I'd managed to get laid back in town, but poor Greg was an ugly turd even those days. . . . I'm so tired and muddled I even think, Well, I'm wearing gloves, perhaps it wouldn't count . . . but I say again politely, 'No thank you, Greg.' "

Jamie looked at Gregory. He was bright red, even his scalp

under his close-cropped silver hair. The crew was starting to shift uneasily. Just the hint of something like that on a ship was dangerous—in the navy Jamie had known it to end in murder.

"Pretty soon," Kell continued, "Greg's kind of rustling around. I hear him unzip his pants. I'm jolted wide awake at that, wide awake and drunk, becoming somewhat nervous, thinking, What the hell?

"And all of a sudden he grabs my hand, puts it on him—and it's up, and hard and *cold!* I'm paralyzed with shock . . . you know how it is, your first time.

" 'Here,' he says, 'hold it while I take a piss' and rolls off the mattress. And I realize I've still got it! It's froze and broken off!

"Well, lads, you never heard such a yell as I let out as I threw the thing across the room.

"And then Greg says, quite mildly, 'I hope you didn't ruin that sausage, Kelly.' "

Kell paused. The whole room roared with laughter. Greg actually fell off his chair. Jamie laughed as hard as he had the first time he'd heard it, long ago.

After a bit, when they had quieted down, Kell finished up his story.

"The sun came out the next day, we got our bearings, and made it back without too much trouble. And it's a good thing, too, because I tell you lads, I'd have starved before I ate that sausage."

Up in the bow of the ship, on watch, Jamie didn't mind the cold. He could look at the waves for hours, not really thinking about anything. The vast expanse of sea was peace to him.

He liked night watch, too. He always volunteered. You got

to sleep late . . . and the ocean seemed different then, like a woman with the lights turned low, familiar but yet strange. . . .

He recognized the footsteps coming up behind him, so he didn't bother to turn.

Kell leaned on the rail next to him. They remained silent for a while.

"Care for a nip, Jamie?" Kell pulled a pint of whiskey from his heavy pea jacket.

"I'm on watch."

Kell took a long swallow.

"Weather's changing. Look at the haze around the moon."

Jamie didn't tell him he already knew that—he felt it in the ocean, the way it was slapping the sides of the ship, like a person with the jitters. But it made Kell nuts when Jamie said he could feel things from the water. Kell always said the only way to know the weather was the sky. And they both preferred instruments. . . .

He turned his back to the wind, huddled to light up a cigarette.

"Jesus, Jamie, you still smoking those Indian bedis? You'll have no lungs left the time you're my age."

"You really think I'll make it to your age?"

"I don't think you'll make it another week, if this hostility between you and Greg continues. It's got me troubled, lad."

"It don't trouble me." Jamie shrugged and faced the sea again.

"Greg's being patient for my sake, but he'll not stomach insolence. He had to take too much as a lad. And he's not a man to run afoul of."

"I hate this fucking job," Jamie said. "I'm not a fucking deckhand."

"You're getting paid five times as much as the captain is, that ought to ease your pride somewhat."

"Look, it was okay when we were on that ship where everybody knew what was going on—but half these guys are honest. Who's gonna believe that if we all get caught?"

"I've never known you to shy away from danger, Jamie. That time we double-crossed Cahill's brother with the Philippine whores—we'd have been shark bait and you damn well knew it and laughed."

"I'll take my own risks. I don't mind that. You said we'd quit two trips ago."

"For God and country, Jamie. And you do owe me."

"Look, what's going on in Ireland's lasted a couple of hundred years. It'll still be going on a hundred years from now. Can't you guys find something else to think about?"

"No," Kell said. "And I've told you, you can't understand unless you've been bred to it, born to it, have it taint every breath you draw."

Kell sipped some more whiskey. Jamie muttered, "My nerves are shot, Kell. I keep thinking about what'll happen if some of the crew find what's in the cargo. We'll have to fight each other. I knew what I was getting into when I signed on . . . but some of the rest of them . . ."

"Loyalty to your crewmates over the job, a fine thing, Jamie. But each man chooses where his loyalty lies. Sometimes the thing you're fighting for is not what it seems. . . . For all my fine war record, I haven't got a country—don't be begrudging me my God."

"I keep forgetting you were in the war, Kell. It seems so long ago."

"Seems like yesterday to me. And I was younger than you are now. It goes so fast, Jamie . . ."

"What the fuck were you serving with the English for, anyway?"

"Well, Jamie, I was serving in the British merchant marine when the MI-6 hauls me in for a little talk.

"'Quinn,' they say, 'since Ireland's staying neutral in this, many take it that some Irishmen are not. If a man with your background decided to slip the Nazis a few favors no one would be surprised, especially them. And if we told you what secrets to slip it could be to our advantage.'

"'No thanks,' I says. 'I'm serving where I am.'

"I'd found my sea home, Jamie; you know what I'm talking about. And the cargo ships were in every bit as much danger as the battleships, only we had no weapons. I was doing as much or more duty than I owed.

"'You've got nothing on me,' I says, 'so I'll be on my merry way.'

"They could have had many things on me, of course, but I was slippery at birth, the midwife couldn't hold me, as my poor mother used to say."

Kell took another drink.

"'Yes,' they says, 'but Kevin and Tim have been naughty lads, sorry to say, we've had to lock them up. If you were to change your mind about helping us, we might change ours about how long they stay there.'

"Well, my heart sank at that, Jamie. I'd been planning to get them berths with me, I'd already made a few contacts, I was just waiting for them to come of age—"

"These were your brothers, Kell?"

"Yes. Had three—for many years it seemed strange to me not to have a snotty wee bro underneath my feet—

"Anyway, I never had much hope for Kevin. A British gaol

is no place to nurse bad lungs, and his were half gone then . . .
but Tim was tough as leather, just turned fifteen, I thought perhaps . . .

"They also had a nice piece of leverage on my old pal
Greg, our dads were in cahoots together . . ." Kell sipped some
more.

"The things Greg and I were asked to do . . . if we had to
kill, we didn't kill in the heat of battle. I hope you never know
what it's like, being asked to do things like that, and come home
to find you're still scum to the country who asked you to do
them . . . but I've never regretted it. You can't regret experience.
It got me out of Ireland, for one thing. Gave me an education—
not a book education, but I learned what I was good at. Finding
people's weak points, how much to press those weak points, how
to apply a leverage to a fraction. Making contacts—I made a lot
of contacts, Jamie. It's a wise thing to be generous at the right
times. There's time to give as well as take. The taking is better
for it, after. People remember their debts."

"That's for goddamn sure," Jamie said. He wouldn't be in this
mess now, except for owing Kell. It ticked him off, thinking Kell
would use him like he'd use anyone else—though he'd known it
all along.

"Well, I was luckier than some. The gift I discovered has
proved very useful since. Others found they had a talent for
killing and no one would give them a medal for it after. Although it can still be quite useful."

Jamie suddenly thought of Gregory—a harebrained young
scamp, Kell said, and now he, too, had a useful gift.

Jamie looked at his face in the moonlight. He rarely saw Kell
look his age. And rarely saw him drunk, though he often saw
him drink.

"So what happened to your brothers?"

Kell was quiet for a few minutes.

"They're all dead now. I was the only one who lived past five-and-twenty. And I the eldest . . . Kevin died in prison. Tim was beat to death by the guards. But it took three of them and they had to cuff him first—

"You know, the first time I saw you, Jamie, I was strongly reminded of Tim. Perhaps because you were fighting. It was one of his favorite pastimes, too. You're really nothing alike, though. . . . You're sunny enough if people let you alone. No, truly, I love you for your own sake, Jamie."

Jamie was forced into a grin. Then he said, "You said three, Kell?"

"Yes. Michael tried to walk home from the pub in a blizzard. A sweet lad, but always muddled, especially after what happened to Kevin and Tim . . .

"If it's all the same to you we'll not bring it up again. It's hard to go on with lines tuggin' at your heart, best to cut loose and be free to sail. . . . I do miss Kevin though. He was a grand talker, Jamie. I can't hold a candle to poor Kevin. . . ."

Jamie suddenly thought: What we're doing, it's getting to Kell, too. It's making him remember stuff. It's time to quit; he needs to more than I do.

"Well, Jamie, I came up here to relieve you. You'd best be getting back."

"Ol' Frozen Dick would have your balls, old pal or not, he found you on watch in this shape. Go sleep it off. I'll take your watch, too. Nothin' better to do."

Gregory did run a tight ship, Jamie had to give him that.

"Now, Jamie," Kell paused, surprised. "I do believe you're right, Jamie, I am drunk. I had no notion . . ."

He hugged Jamie's shoulders. "This is the last run, boy, I promise. Will you listen to me about Greg, though, lad?"

He gave Jamie a fierce shake, half affection, half warning.

"Yeah," Jamie said. "Sure."

There was a storm coming up. And Jamie knew any delay getting this damn boat into the damned port and getting rid of this goddamn fucking cargo would cause his nerves to snap.

What if some of the cargo came loose? What if they got into serious trouble at sea?

Ol' First Mate Gregory would sink the ship before he'd let someone find out what she carried. His guys weren't just ready to kill, they were plenty ready to die.

If this endless run ever got over with, Jamie was through. He'd have enough money for once; he wouldn't owe Kell anything.

He was going to New Orleans, with Kell or without him.

Jamie stood at the railing, smoking, wrapped up in his rain slicker. He'd been busy battening for an hour. The sea was starting to roll, the wind getting worse, the rain starting to fall hard. Soon he'd have to go in.

Jamie hated storms, having to go below, getting bounced all over your bunk, needing a smoke and no way to have one.

It had to be very, very bad before Jamie would get seasick.

"Jamie!" Steve ran up, grasping the slippery rails, panting for breath. He hadn't even put his slicker on. "Jamie, I just found . . ."

Jamie wasn't ready.

"Shut the fuck up!" he said desperately. Steve read the knowledge in his eyes.

"But Jamie," he said, "don't you know what they'll use those guns for?"

"You didn't see anything! You got that?"

"It's not war, Jamie, they use them to murder!"

"For God's sake, Steve, shut the fuck up!"

"Well, lads"—Gregory joined them—"looks like a rough time ahead."

Swiftly he clamped a hand over Steve's mouth, drove the knife in twice, once in each lung with a twist, hoisted him overboard.

Steve didn't have time to bleed. He barely made a splash as he disappeared soundlessly in the rough water.

Gone.

Jamie's heart stood still. Then slowly he straightened, turned.

"It's a sad thing, to lose a man in a storm, but once in a while we do," said Gregory.

Jamie met his steel-eyed glance.

"For God and country, Jamie," Greg's voice raised against the wind.

"For Jamie Sommers," Jamie answered.

It was the best thing he could have said. For you could see he had no country, that he knew there was no God.

New Orleans
JANUARY 1965

"I was robbed?" Jamie said uncertainly. He didn't remember being robbed, but he must have been, to be this low on money.

"Now, Jamie, why would anyone want to be robbin' you?

When you're giving it away? Any girl who said she'd fucked you, any man who claimed to be your pal—especially if he had white powder. Drinks on Jamie, all up and down Bourbon Street. You've spent money like the proverbial drunken sailor, Jamie—drank most of it, put quite a bit up your nose. I understand there were parties, in the fancy hotel, before they kicked you out."

Jamie felt too shaky to argue. He needed a drink, a snort, but couldn't get the strength together to go out and hunt for it.

The dealers were no longer hunting him.

"When's the last time you ate something, lad?"

"Leave me alone," Jamie said. "Quit nursemaiding me."

"You look like shit—I leave for three weeks and come back to find you like this—"

Jamie was trembling from too much drink and cocaine, emaciated from too little food, bleary-eyed from no sleep, too much sex; he carried bruises from four fights he could barely remember.

He felt like shit.

"No use brooding about young Malloy," Kell said impatiently.

If you cried over every tragedy the Troubles had caused, there'd be a whole new ocean, Kell thought. A sad thing, but the lad had first run to Jamie, who supposedly knew nothing—what else could Gregory do?

And Jamie had been sullen, silent, abrasive ever since.

And now this mad attempt to drink and drug himself happy—Kell had seen such soul-sick men before, they could be dangerous.

If Jamie couldn't pull himself together soon, they'd have to part ways.

"Ain't brooding," Jamie said, trying to remember if he'd hid any money somewhere.

"No need blaming Gregory—you yourself knifed a fellow not long ago, over a simple jailhouse romance, for all I know."

"Me? That guy, he was gonna . . ." Jamie shuddered at the memory of the Algerian's sweaty, heavy body, his obscene stare always following Jamie's every movement. "Besides, who cares? He didn't have . . ."

Jamie stopped.

"Didn't have what? Didn't have a mother? A wife and child at home? Did you stop to ask him, Jamie?" Kell took a breath. "Or did you do what had to be done?"

Jamie closed his eyes. *"Don't you know what they'll use those guns for?"*

Jamie would wipe out the memory of Steve's face with anything at hand but could always hear his voice.

"How much was in my wallet?" When he heard, he said, "Oh fuck."

"Well, if that's what you're after you'll have to use some persuasion. You'll not be buying it for a while."

Jamie dropped his head into his hands, rubbing his hair back. The cold rain beat ceaselessly on the window. It was always raining now.

He was sick of everything. There wasn't any reason for anything. The why of it all overwhelmed him.

"Listen, Jamie, I'm going up to Hawkes Harbor, Delaware. There's a widow there I've a hankering to visit. It's a quiet little town, uncanny kind of place, strange, but you could rest up there."

"The widow's rich, huh?"

"No need to be cynical, lad, but yes. And very lovely."

"And she'll be glad to see you?"

"I can make her glad to see me. If not, she might give me a generous farewell gift."

Hawkes Harbor. Uncanny, huh? Sounded like something Kell would say—Kell was tripping over ghosts in the Philippines, paying off witches in Africa, who knew what he meant by "uncanny," applied to some little backwater hole?

But at least it was a plan. Jamie had no plan.

"So, how'd the Caribbean bank deal go?" Jamie asked. "You leave a lot of money there?"

Jamie was starting, just a little, to be glad to see Kell. Although he hadn't missed him at all these last three weeks, had thought he didn't care if he ever saw him again.

If he would just quit nursemaiding. Quit mentioning Steve Malloy.

"Some, not as much as I hoped."

Jamie never realized, because Kell didn't himself, that there would never, ever be as much money as Kell hoped.

Once Kell put money in the bank—and he had accounts all over the world—it was gone for him; he had to do with what was at hand.

The backbreaking, soul-deadening poverty Kellen Quinn grew up in made Jamie's life at the orphanage look like a stint at a luxury resort.

There would never be enough money for Kell—though if he'd thought to add all his accounts together he'd be pleasantly surprised. He was worth close to half a million dollars.

"So you'll come with me, boy? I'm going to go by train."

Kell, too, was a little soul-sick. They'd lived hard, these last years. Young Malloy's murder bothered him, more than he'd admit. Maybe Lydia would be more than just an easy touch for a stake, another profitable leverage.

It would be nice to have a home at my age, Kell thought.

"You go ahead," Jamie said. "I'll get a job, a berth up to Dover. I'll meet you up there."

"Trains . . ." Kell began.

"I don't want to owe you nothing!" Jamie snapped. "And I want to be at sea."

"All right, Jamie," Kell said. "I'll go on ahead."

Jamie drained the water glass sitting next to the bed. He felt a little ashamed. . . .

"So who's widow is this, anyway?"

"Mine," Kell said. "Mine."

Leaving for Hawkes Hall

Terrace View Asylum, Delaware
OCTOBER 1967

Dr. McDevitt watched Jamie repair the leak in the kitchen sink. He was thorough, methodical, chose his tools carefully.

He wasn't fast, but very careful. Jamie had put a door back on its hinges, fixed the hot-water heater, and gave an opinion, which turned out to be correct, on the television.

Jamie had watched the TV repairman at work, talked to him occasionally. It was one of the days when he'd bothered to dress and the repairman took him to be an attendant and enjoyed explaining what he was doing—until Nurse Whiting came by with Jamie's afternoon meds.

Then the repairman got nervous and clammed up, like many people did when they realized they were talking to a mental patient. Jamie eventually wandered off.

Dr. McDevitt sighed at the memory. He would have felt for any patient, but Jamie so rarely tried to relate to anyone. . . .

"Where did you learn these skills, Jamie? The navy?" The doctor felt a little guilty, using a patient like this (the janitor Albert was often missing or drunk or both), but the work had a calming effect on Jamie and seemed to alleviate his depression, and he was glad to help each time he was asked. The doctor decided it was therapy.

"No." Jamie's voice came from under the sink. "Not the navy. Concentrated on navigation, instruments, seamanship in the navy. That and guns. I was in the South China Sea, it was before 'Nam got so hot, but even then you saw a lot of guns there.

"No, I went to a vo-tech high school. It was a good place. They made sure you could use everything—like I'm not good at reading, but I can read maps and technical fine. Not good at math, but I can chart a course, translate money. My handwriting's real bad, but I can keep a log so you can read it. Plumbing, carpentry, small-engine repair, auto mechanics—my wood-shop teacher had a fit when I joined the navy, he wanted me to go into cabinetry, but all I ever wanted was to go to sea. I was a fuckin' straight-A student, which'll surprise you. Almost got kicked out twice, because of fighting, that probably won't . . . that ought to hold it."

He slid out from under the cabinet.

"Jamie, I'm not surprised only because you have told me you had something of a violent nature in the past—I certainly wouldn't deduce that from my own personal experience with you."

Jamie lay flat on his back for a minute. "Yeah. See, Grenville did that for me. Once I started working for him, I was thinking, Now I really know how it feels to hurt, so I don't want to hurt anybody. I started thinking about what I was doing. Like when I was running guns, I thought about getting caught, if I was going to get paid, if those gangsters were just gonna drop me overboard some night—but I never did think about what the guns were used for, till it was too late. How many people they'd kill. Me and Kell did a lot of stuff I ain't too proud of . . . hell, it wasn't Kell's fault, I did plenty on my own. Now I try every day to have nothing to be sorry about."

"Mr. Hawkes did this for you? How?"

"I can't remember exactly. He gave me a chance to reform, I remember that." He sat up.

"Oh shit." He rubbed at his right shoulder. "Goddamn fuckin'—" His swearing demonstrating a skill he *had* learned in the navy, while tears welled up in his eyes.

Dr. McDevitt went to the intercom and ordered a pain reliever.

"Your shoulder hurts?"

"My whole back." Jamie grimaced, rocking a little. "That goddamn cop did a number on me, all right. And I wasn't doin' nothing. . . ."

Jamie cried for a few minutes, gulped his pill between sobs. Eventually he quit trembling.

"It's a good thing I'm left-handed. . . . You think I'll ever get well? My back, I mean. I know you got your doubts about my mind."

"Jamie, I think mentally you can improve, and physically you will get better.

"I wouldn't be surprised, though, if your shoulder always gives you trouble. You had extensive damage both to bone and muscle. Did they ever explain that to you at the infirmary?"

"You mean, at Eastern State? I can't remember the infirmary, don't even remember the ward much, now."

Keep your head down, your mouth shut, and you won't get kicked. That was what he remembered. Always hunting for a safe corner . . .

"And your physical therapist here, what does she tell you?"

"That I'm the biggest pussy about pain she's ever seen, a ten-year-old could take it better, next time she'll give me something to cry about—"

There was a sudden sharp crack, and Dr. McDevitt looked at his broken pencil. He put the pieces in his pocket and took out another, freshly sharpened. His coat and shirt pockets were filled with pencils, both whole and broken.

The patients joked about it, as well he knew. "I made Dr. Mac snap three times today," he'd overhear. "How about you?"

"Doc? Hey, don't take it so serious. She's right. Come on, don't look like that."

"Jamie, I am so sorry. We'll find you another therapist right away. You have an abnormally low pain tolerance, I thought that had been explained to her."

He made a note to fire the therapist. If there was one thing Dr. McDevitt prided himself on, it was the humane conditions at Terrace View. And the one thing he could not tolerate was cruelty.

Jamie's low pain tolerance had puzzled him from the beginning.

Dr. McDevitt at one point had even thought about ordering neurological tests to determine the cause of this, but decided against it. The number of mu receptors any one person possessed determined their pain tolerance—you were born with it, like red hair or freckles. Dr. McDevitt had no idea how this could be altered physically.

"Have you always been like this, Jamie?"

"Doc," Jamie said, the pain reliever relaxing him, "I'm tryin' to cooperate, never talked so much in my life, but sometimes I get the feeling you ain't hearin' me. No, I haven't been like this all my life. I never used to cry, ever. I saw a friend get killed right in front of me, and I didn't bat an eye. Well, that time the shark skinned me and I had to steer us outta there, I might have bitched around a little—but if I'd been like this on a ship I'dve been tied to an anchor and tossed overboard. People would think I was a Jonah. I coulda never got into the navy. . . ." He stopped suddenly. "What am I gonna do, if I ever get outta here? I can't go back to sea."

The tears came welling up again as Jamie plunged back into despair.

"Jamie, I'll gladly replace Albert with you, if you ever need a job. Or write any letter of recommendation—once you've recovered, of course."

Jamie was quiet for a few minutes.

"I used to think maybe Grenville would want me back. I did a lot of work for him. Fixed up Hawkes Hall. He said I did a good job."

"Grenville Hawkes? Perhaps he will. You know he's paying your bills here."

And Louisa Kahne is giving him an obscene discount, the doctor added to himself.

"Well, he was always good to me. Giving me a job when everybody told him not to, he even got me to quit smoking and drinking. But I think he forgot all about me."

"I want to hear how you met him. But now, do you have any idea why you are so sensitive to pain? When did this happen to you?"

Jamie gingerly got to his feet and eased into a kitchen chair.

"I think it was when I got sick at the boardinghouse . . . that's when a lot of things changed for me. That's about the time I met Grenville . . . me and Kell split up for good . . . Things were never the same with me and Kell, after I went to work for Grenville. I think maybe it hurt his feelings, that I didn't talk it over with him first . . . but then he got convinced I was pulling some kinda scam on Grenville, ripping him off somehow, and wasn't cutting him in. Hell, I wouldn't scam Grenville. I'd be scared to, for one thing, he's the smartest guy I ever knew, he'd figure it out in no time. But why would I want to, him being nice to me like that? I was sick of scams. I couldn't make Kell understand." Jamie paused. "Anyway, everything that happened about then: Grenville, splitting up with Kell, this pain crap, all that gets mixed up. I don't know what caused what. . . ."

"Maybe talking would help set it straight." Dr. McDevitt discreetly looked at his watch. He was officially off work, his wife would be upset if he were late again. Then, Jamie had fixed the leak. . . . He turned the page in his notebook.

"I got real sick in Hawkes Harbor. That's unusual for me. I never get sick. I was in the hospital in San Diego, but that was from a knife fight while I was still in the navy—it don't count as sick. Got a coral cut in the French Pollies, but healed up pretty fast; sometimes those get real nasty.

"Never got malaria. Kell used to have a bout of it once a year, it really knocked him out. Never got the clap or nothin'; Kell was amazed, but I let him think I never used a rubber. I never was that stupid—those movies they show in the navy, you never want to screw again. For fifteen minutes, anyway. Ten if you have shore leave.

"Did take some chances, though. Guess I was lucky, too."

Dr. McDevitt agreed with that, after all he'd heard. But he remembered Jamie's blood work quite well—no venereal disease, true, but still something odd. . . . He shook his head. Blood was not his specialty . . . he focused again on Jamie's story.

"Oh yeah, once, in Mozambique, east coast of Africa, me and Kell both came down with dysentery. Man, that was hell. We were fighting over who was the most miserable. Then Kell got up this contest . . ."

Jamie grinned faintly at the memory.

Dr. McDevitt looked down at his notes, hoping to be spared the details of the contest.

"But other than some motherfuckin' hangovers, being too doped or drunk, I never get sick.

"Musta caught some weird flu or something in Hawkes Harbor. I never felt so awful. Too weak to move, couldn't eat or drink, I know I have bad dreams now but they can't be worse than what I was having then—strange, sick shit, too weird to even talk about."

Jamie rubbed the back of his neck. "My landlady said I got up and ran around at night, but maybe I'm remembering that wrong because I couldn't have, I was so weak. Kell even called a doctor. . . .

"What did the doctor say?"

Jamie looked puzzled.

"The doctor Kell called to the boardinghouse?"

"Oh. He said I'd lost some blood—so I'd been in a bar fight, guy cut me with a bottle, it was no reason to be that sick—doctors make mistakes, that's what I told Kell. No offense."

Jamie took a breath, and Dr. McDevitt saw he was feeling the effect of the tranquilizer contained in the pain medication.

"Even Kell wanted me out of Hawkes Harbor. I'd become damn odd, he said. . . ."

"Jamie, I want you to think about this, and we'll discuss it tomorrow. Everything, the town, Mr. Hawkes, your illness—I have a feeling it's important. Now I want you to rest. Come to my office in the morning after breakfast."

"Okay." Jamie sighed sleepily. "But you better send for me. I'll probably forget. . . ."

He left to take a nap. And within an hour woke up screaming.

The next afternoon Dr. McDevitt sat down with his tape recorder. He hit the Rewind button, and the tape whirled backward.

He had some of Jamie's story but wanted to make sure of a few things. And there was that odd tone in Jamie's voice, an occasional hesitance that almost amounted to a question mark. As if what he was saying puzzled him, too.

He was sure Jamie wasn't consciously lying, but no doubt he was confused.

Dr. McDevitt hit the Play button and settled back with his notes.

"You ever been to Hawkes Harbor, Doc? I'm not surprised. Not much there for visitors, nice scenery but not great, some history stuff. It gets a few tourists.

"The Hawkes family founded the town of Hawkes Harbor. Hundreds of years ago. I ain't too good at history, but it was real early, like when America was still part of England. Everywhere you go in that town, there's the name Hawkes. They still own most of it, the mills, the shipping and trucking line, a munitions plant.

"Kell moved into one of the Hawkes family mansions. Turns out he had married a Hawkes, during the war, she had been a Red Cross nurse or something, run away from her rich family to see the world. I guess things didn't work out too well, he probably went through her money too fast or chased one skirt too many; he never told me the details. They couldn't divorce, being Catholics and everything, so she paid him off, so she could go home to her family, made him give her a death certificate so she could be a widow. I told you Kell knows a real good forgery guy, right?

"Well, this blackmail scam was going pretty good when I got there. He was supposedly a long-lost brother of the dead husband, and making a lot out of it. Money, clothes, I think he was going to try to marry her again, except she was already engaged to some hotshot business tycoon. Kell had his hands full with that guy, all right.

"Anyway, when I got to Hawkes Harbor, it pissed me off, Kell getting to live in that fancy mansion, me being stuck at the boardinghouse. He'd pulled that kind of shit with me before. It was a nice boardinghouse, though . . . Katie worked there. . . .

"You gotta understand, Doc, I was in bad shape then. Got myself fucked up on cocaine in New Orleans, blew a big wad of money, and I was drinking heavy, trying to come down off it. On my way to Hawkes Harbor I got kicked off a ship I was crewing, first time that ever happened to me. Then got jailed in Ocean City—assault, but the other guy was drunk too, no charges—yeah, I was in a real good mood by the time I got there . . .

"And here's old Kellen Quinn, the dapper Irish gentleman, hob-nobbin' with the town elite, with his fancy friends in one of those fancy houses. Not that they liked him, though. The Hawkes are real suspicious of strangers. Hell, they still won't have much to do with Grenville, and he's related to them.

"Anyway, I barged in on them a couple of times, pretending to visit Kell, they had to ask me to dinner, those kind of people are ruled by good manners.

"I'm not, so you can probably guess what kind of asshole I was there. Drank their brandy, came on to the niece, Barbara—her father, Richard Hawkes, Kell's brother-in-law, made remarks about how most people only ate *one* dinner at a sitting. He hated Kell being there, he didn't know what Kellen had on his sister but he suspected something . . . you can imagine how he felt about me. He was funny, in a way, though, said some sharp things. I sure don't blame them for wanting me out of there. I was making Kell damn nervous, too . . ."

Dr. McDevitt turned up the volume; he wanted to make sure of his own comments.

"You're quite agitated today, Jamie. Are you sure you want to go on?"

"Yeah, why not? I can walk around while I'm talking, can't I? You let me before."

"You received your morning meds?"

"Hell, yeah. You know me, I'll take anything you'll give me—it's getting dark out?"

"No, it's just clouding up, perhaps it'll storm soon. . . . It's just ten in the morning, Jamie."

"Oh."

[a long silence]

"So you had no friends in Hawkes Harbor?"

"Oh yeah, I did. Trisha, the landlady's little kid, her and Ricky Hawkes. They're about eleven. Ricky hated living in the mansion, there was nobody his age there and he didn't even get to go to school, had a tutor. He was hanging around with Trisha a lot; she's a sharp little imp. Katie's little sister. Different last names, though, Mrs. Pivens been married twice. The kids and me used to sit on the landing outside the second story of the boardinghouse, look at Hawkes Island. Me and them were pals."

Hawkes Harbor, Delaware
FEBRUARY 1965

"So you guys are saying there's pirates' loot buried over on the island? Why don't you just go dig it up?"

"Nobody goes on the island. It's haunted."

"And it's not an island. It's a peninsula. See? There's the land bridge."

"Smarty. But Jamie, nobody has lived there for a jillion years."

"That weird woman is living at the Lodge. I heard she was a witch."

"The Lodge isn't exactly on the island. Anyway, she's some kind of teacher, studying history. We have some really cool history here, Jamie. Like the first colony, they disappeared off the island without a trace, like the colony at Roanoke. And the Indians were weird, too."

"Well, I don't know what Roanoke is, but the pirate stuff is interesting. What else do you know about that?"

"Don't tell anyone. Cross your heart and hope to die?"

"Sure."

"There's caves on the other side of the island. That's where the treasure's buried."

"No shit? Well, let's go take a look sometime."

"No! The whole island is haunted! It's evil! Jamie, swear you'll never go there!"

"Come on, relax. Okay, okay, I swear. So what kind of treasure, you think?"

"So the children were your only friends in Hawkes Harbor?" Dr. McDevitt asked.

"Katie was always nice to me. . . . Well, my landlady, Mrs. Pivens, she liked me. Don't ask me why—'cept she had a son about my age, he turned out bad. I guess she wanted to believe guys like us were good, deep down somewhere."

Hawkes Harbor, Delaware
FEBRUARY 1965

"So, Mrs. Pivens, I hear that island is haunted."

"Nonsense. I'd think a bright young man like you would know better than to pay attention to children. The first Hawkes mansion is still standing there, it was abandoned during the Civil War, and no one has lived there since. But that's convenience, nothing else."

"How about the pirates' loot? The kids were saying . . ."

"Well, there is some truth to that. The first Hawkes was said to be a pirate, and of course they roamed this shoreline. And some would say the Hawkes are pirates still! Ha ha! Tightfisted buggers. . . . So your Irish friend, they say he's got his sights set high. . . . Here have another cookie, Jamie, tell me what's going on up on the hill."

Dr. McDevitt fast-forwarded through another long silence. Jamie had paced the room, wiping his palms on his robe, always glancing at the window.

The storm clouds had darkened, giving the sky a look of twilight.

"You were going to tell me how you met Grenville Hawkes," the doctor's voice resumed.

Jamie had looked at him with mute appeal, like someone stricken dumb.

Dr. McDevitt said, "Can you remember the first thing he said to you?"

"Yeah. He asked w-w-what y-year it was."

"Didn't you think that a rather odd question?"

"No. Why should I? He didn't have a watch on."

"You said he asked you what year it was."

"No I didn't! I said he asked me for the time!"

"All right, Jamie—perhaps we should continue this later, you seem upset today."

"Ain't upset!"

Dr. McDevitt turned off the machine. A clap of thunder, a sudden power surge ended the tape there. The lights had come back on immediately, to reveal Jamie huddled on the floor. The doctor knelt beside him; he heard quite clearly:

"Let me be dead.

"Let me be dead.

"Let me be dead."

Hawkes Island, Delaware
MARCH 1965

Let me be dead.

Jamie lay on the floor of the secret room in the cave. His bones brittle from the cold, he shook uncontrollably, his teeth chattering so hard his jaws hurt. The back of his head, his shoulders ached from being slammed up against the wall of the cave, being pinned by the throat.

Let me be dead.

The pain was incredible. The wound in his throat burned like he'd been scalded with acid; somehow that acid had entered his bloodstream and seemed to be gnawing his blood vessels, his very heart. . . .

The worst was the memory of the cold greedy mouth on his neck, the sickening crunching noise as the fangs drove through his flesh, the sensation of being eaten alive, the small inhuman sounds of satisfaction It made—as hard as his heart had been pumping, it wasn't enough—the suction left a bruise from his jaw to his collarbone.

It happened as fast as lightning. . . . It seemed to take forever. . . . Jamie didn't expect to live through it, and now he was so sorry he had. . . .

He had dropped to his knees and vomited when the Thing released him and the vomit in his bruised, swollen throat almost choked him. Then he keeled over on his side, and now lay quivering and panting like a half-killed rabbit before a beast of prey.

He had his eyes shut tight, but water gushed from them. It was so cold. It was so cold. . . .

Let me be dead.

If he were dead he would no longer see those red eyes glaring up at him from the coffin. He'd been so lucky, he'd thought, to stumble on the boulder, so obviously blocking an entrance . . . he'd taken little notice of the ancient symbol painted on the rock . . . X marks the spot, he'd thought, and when he levered the boulder to the side, and the X became a cross, he still did not guess. . . . Lucky he'd brought his tools with him—the chest was full of coins, the old lock rusted . . .

And the chained coffin . . . obviously containing something valuable, he gloated . . .

For who would chain a coffin . . . ?

Then there was that moment when the universe had shifted for Jamie, when he pried open the lid—for a spilt second his mind had fumbled for a word, he wanted a word, there was a word—

Then the iron grip seized him and it was too late. And faster than was humanly possible, he was slammed against the wall. The horror of the moment, when It grasped his hair, pulled back his head, and he realized what was happening . . . this is really happening . . . his eyes grew heavy, as the Vampire's saliva drugged him into compliance, lessened coagulates in his bloodstream, entered his nervous system to attack the mu receptors . . . Jamie's pain tolerance was destroyed in seconds, never to return.

Then, after, It let him fall, as if disgusted. . . .

Jamie didn't want to wake. He wanted to be dead.

"What is the year?"

Oh, God . . . It could speak . . . and had a voice like Death. . . .

The year? What year? What did It mean? Jamie's mind raced almost incoherently.

"N-n-nineteen s-s-sixty-five," he heard himself sob, surprised to find he could answer, finding it impossible not to.

"Nineteen hundred and sixty-five?"

Suddenly It grabbed him by the upper arm, jerking him to his feet, strode out of the cave, dragging Jamie behind as easily as if he were a rag doll. The inhuman strength . . . Jamie stumbled over small monuments, the headstones of some long-forgotten cemetery, bumping from one to another, scrambling to keep on his feet. The smell of rotting leaves, mildew, age-old sorrows . . . death.

It went swiftly through the old graveyard, not glancing at the tombstones, Jamie stumbling and gasping in Its wake.

It stopped in the clearing at the edge of the cemetery, Jamie's sobbing breath the only sound. . . . The frigid dew soaked through his socks. Bone-chilled, exhausted, crazed, he could barely raise his head.

Down below the windswept hill, the lights of Hawkes Harbor sparkled on the edge of the sea, like a cluster of stars in the night. The Thing stood silent.

Jamie would have fallen, weak from loss of blood, and shock, but It held him—his arm would be black with bruises for days.

Jamie's heart skipped wildly when It turned to him. He saw It clearly for the first time. Tall, gaunt, and silver-skinned, the dark and depthless eyes . . . and perhaps the most grotesque thing of all . . . still . . . a human face . . .

"And in 1965—do the Hawkes still rule Hawkes Harbor?"

In the few remaining minutes before the dawn, the Vampire's many questions answered, the best that Jamie could, It left him, the final sentence pronounced:

"This coming night I will summon you. And you will obey."

Jamie stumbled out to a grotesque dawn in Hawkes Harbor, to find what an ugly, harsh thing sunlight was, what a hideous sound the seagulls made.

The ocean made him nauseous.

When he found himself back at the boardinghouse, somehow, delirious, twisting in his bed, he kept begging, "Don't let it be dark. Don't let it be dark. Don't let it be dark."

He would have begged for death, but he knew It wouldn't let him be dead.

Terrace View Asylum, Delaware
AUGUST 1967

"Are you feeling better today, Jamie?"

"Yeah. I don't know what happened. I ain't usually scared of storms."

"Let's see—you got sick at the boardinghouse and Kell Quinn called a doctor. Is that correct?

"Yeah. Kell thought I'd been out on a spree or something. . . .

(*"Good God, lad, you look like death! I've searched every bar and whorehouse for a hundred miles around. . . . Jamie, look at me, boy! What's happened to you?"*)

"But I hadn't. I was just sick. You know, Doc, laying there sick like that, I got to thinking what my life had been like. How I'd never amounted to much, some of the fucked-up stuff I'd done."

"Your illness made you remorseful?"

"Yeah. I wanted to start again, somehow—atone."

"Atone?"

"Yeah. If I could atone there was hope . . . I made up my mind, I was going to change, when I went to work for Grenville."

"That's when you met Mr. Hawkes?"

"Yeah. His car broke down on the road. He hired me when I fixed it. I had nowhere else to go."

Hawkes Harbor, Delaware
FEBRUARY 1965

"But why do you need to leave here, Jamie?"

"I told ya, Trish. I'm going to be working at Hawkes Hall now."

"I still don't know why you have to live there."

"It's part of the deal. Room and board."

"Well . . . Jamie? Did you know you're shaking?"

"Yeah. I need a drink. Go on, scram, I can't get things done. . . ."

Back in the boardinghouse, packing to leave it forever, Jamie looked out the window, at the blank, black wall where the future used to be. Nothing. No hope, no nothing, but that voice in his brain.

"I'm comin' ," he muttered. *"I hear you."*

He paused on the outside landing, looking across the harbor where the land was darker than night. A small light, like a tiny star on a vast black sky flickered.

He was so frightened . . . the black tide was rising swiftly around him, pulling him into dark waters. . . . What's going to happen now?

The summons was stronger now, impatient, and Jamie could smell in the cold sea wind the faint stench of the tomb.

Oh yeah, I hear you.

He went swiftly down the steps, took the road to the harbor, the dark path to the bridge. As he walked faster, leaving the lights of town behind, he suddenly remembered the word he'd wished for, when he'd opened the coffin and realized what he'd done . . .

Oh God, he breathed. God. God. God.

But it wasn't God who waited.

New Job

Dr. McDevitt noticed a few new behaviors in Jamie after his last session. He began showing up at mail call, loitering at the edge of eager patients. He could be found on the front-porch lounge every visiting day, anxiously studying each arriving car.

Then finally one day Lee called out, "Mail for Jamie Sommers."

"You're looking well today," Dr. McDevitt said at that same day's session.

"Yeah. I got a letter from Grenville. I had a feeling I was gonna get one, after he visited last week."

"He did?" The doctor knew very well he hadn't—he kept careful records of all the visitors. "I'm sorry I missed him."

"Yeah. But he came late-night Thursday. You weren't here."

The only occurrence out of the usual that happened Thursday evening was some sort of wild animal or bird coming through the opened window of the patients' lounge—Lee had told him it had taken several hours and a major dispensing of sedatives to calm everyone back down.

The doctor only nodded at Jamie's news.

"I'm very glad to hear it. I hope all's well in Hawkes Harbor."

"Well, I don't know about that, but he's got quite a few chores lined up for me when I get out."

Dr. McDevitt looked at his notes, and carefully loosed his grip on his pencil.

"I see."

"I was thinking maybe he forgot all about me. Didn't need me anymore."

"You enjoyed working for him, then?"

"Well . . . it was a little rocky at first. He's one of the colonial Brits, they're real used to servants, and he's kinda eccentric. Strict. Made me nervous I wasn't doing stuff right."

"Yes. So he's British?"

"Yeah, but from Singapore. You can tell the accent's a little weird. Funny, when I went to Boston that time with Kell, I hadn't been in the States in years. I'd forgot how Americans think they're the center of the world. But to tell you the truth, no matter what off-the-map little hellhole, there's some Brit there, drinking his tea and reading his Shakespeare."

"Could I have an example of his . . . 'eccentricity'?"

Jamie paused for a moment. "He had me trapping rats."

"Around his house? That doesn't sound too odd."

"Well, there was a bunch swarming Hawkes Hall when we moved in. But he didn't want me to kill them. I had to use live traps."

"Must have a profound regard for life."

"Yeah. He likes them live."

Jamie fell silent. He brought out his letter—looked up at Dr. McDevitt and grinned.

"You know, Grenville trusted me with money. Even Kellen never did that. He sent me out to buy a car."

"I'm sure you were trustworthy at that point."

"Oh yeah . . ." Jamie looked at his note again. "And he doesn't like . . . lights."

Hawkes Hall, Hawkes Harbor, Delaware
MARCH 1965

It hated electricity—"That fool, Franklin, look what he has wrought."

Jamie, facing life in the derelict Hawkes Hall, thought the goddamn Vampire was fucking nuts sometimes. Resigned, he made up his mind to lanterns, candles, firewood.

In other ways, It wasn't stupid. Pretty damn smart, in fact. It took an inventory of the things It needed and instructed Jamie in how to acquire them.

Within a few weeks, Grenville Hawkes had a new wardrobe— tailor-made at great expense. He'd been an officer in the French and Indian Wars, he chose a military haircut, as becoming an ex-soldier, Jamie doing the best he could. The Vampire had once been a handsome man—and even now, with the shadowed eyes and unhealthy pallor, his height and commanding presence might seem attractive.

Jamie guessed Its age—not counting the time It had spent in the coffin—at close to fifty.

It bought Hawkes Hall.

The property had been listed since World War II; local economy remained depressed, then the death of the realtor, lack of interest, the persistent rumors—all seemed combined to keep the property abandoned.

The Hawkeses themselves had given up on it. They had been pleasantly surprised to find a buyer—some sort of relative?—and too pleased at the cash offer, to make any resistance. They could use a little cash at the moment, and could tell each other solemnly that it was only right to keep the island in the family. And after all, who would have the rundown old place . . . except a daft Englishman? He intended to restore it, so his story went, history was his hobby. Yes, he was quite knowledgeable in antiques. Early American, actually, was a specialty, having always been intrigued by the family stories of the American Hawkes . . .

Numismatics was more than a hobby; it had rivaled his dealings in trade as a source of income. Now, semiretired, still recovering from a tropical fever, there was more than time to indulge these interests—in a better climate, Singapore not the healthiest of places. And more than enough money . . .

The Hawkeses responded politely in the beginning. Had him to dinner. Richard showed him around the property. Lydia had him to tea. Then they shut their doors.

Just your typical snobby rich bastards, Jamie wanted to tell It. But he kept his mouth shut.

"I don't understand," the Vampire said. "The Hawkes have always put an emphasis on family."

"Maybe they don't believe you. You don't much look like the rest of them."

"I researched the records. They are descendants of my brother Charles, who favored my mother's family." He paused. "Charles was somewhat frivolous. Charming, but careless."

It paused. "Apparently my son, William, died without issue."

Jamie made no answer. Sometimes, late at night, when he was repairing the staircase, taking measurements for new flooring, the Vampire would stand at the window and gaze out at the town on the other side of the harbor. It would talk then, reminisce. It had been married twice . . . the first marriage arranged by the families . . . a pleasant girl . . . they had known each other since childhood . . . they had been content, and both doted on the only son, even more so after the twin girls had died of fever at eleven . . . and when It had been a widower for several years, It had met his second wife, Sophia Marie . . . his dear love . . .

It surprised him that the Vampire, with Its strong but subtle cruel streak, who at best must have been a stern man, could go all sticky-moony-candy-assed over this long-lost Sophia Marie. Jamie didn't fool himself, that It was taking him into confidence. It would have talked so to a cat.

It had finally listened to reason, about putting in running water, letting Jamie make the pantry into a crude bathroom.

"You just want it for your own convenience," It snapped. "An unnecessary luxury."

"Yeah, I want it for my own convenience, I ain't looking forward to freezing my ass off in the woods, pissing in a bucket, but I've lived rough before. Two things, here—look how much time it takes, heating up water for a bath. There's plenty of other stuff I could be doing."

"Bathing every day is absurd."

"Well, people do it in this century, especially this country. Showers only take five minutes. And one wouldn't hurt you, either."

"What do you mean?"

Jamie looked down, trembling, but muttered, "What'd ya think I mean?"

The Vampire had a sickening smell to It. Not a heavy moist odor like people, but a dry, nasty scent, like old blood.

And, God, Its foul breath could shrivel flies on a shit hill.

"Look," Jamie went on, when It didn't hit him, "you don't like electricity, fine, it's cute, people think you're eccentric—remember, though, normal people can't hear it—I heard you tell your cousin Richard you couldn't stand the way it sounds—but you don't put in a bathroom, people are going to think you're nuts. They'll start wondering about you. Last thing you need, people wondering about you any more than they have to."

"Yes. I see. You may go ahead."

Funny, the things Jamie expected would most amaze It—airplanes, telephones—made little impact.

"Once you understand the principles of aerodynamics, flying is nothing to be amazed about," It said, after reading one of the books Jamie checked out of the library. "And telephones are far too intrusive. I'll not have one in this house.

"But universal suffrage—an idealist's pipe dream in my day—the free education. I suppose even a lout like you could have taken advantage of it? The abundance and variety of food! In every season!" And, "This rate of taxation would have caused another war in my time."

For a rich guy, It was always griping about prices.

It liked the idea of automobiles, though.

Horses were unreliable, It said. Always losing shoes.

Automobiles. Jamie had given It good advice: "See, you need a Mercedes. You're supposed to be a rich guy from overseas? Well, I been in a lot of places, most have Mercedes, it'd be natural to want one here. I can take the bus over to Georgetown and buy you one. And I can be your chauffeur, you won't need to know how to drive."

"Sometimes I see a glimmer of intelligence in your inept logic," It told him. "But I shall learn to drive."

Good thing It caught on quickly; Jamie's heart would have given out before too long. He hadn't realized all the dangers inherent in driving too slow. Fortunately, having somewhat mastered the skill, enough to satisfy Its vanity, the Vampire preferred to be driven.

Jamie took great pride in the Mercedes. None of the other Hawkes had one. He smirked, remembering their reaction. *They* were still driving Lincolns and Caddies. And none of *them* used a chauffeur.

Grenville had been pleased, too, by the way Jamie had arranged for a fake passport, although It had mocked him for a criminal.

"It comes in handy, you got to admit," Jamie said.

Sometimes, Jamie thought it was like being in on the biggest scam in the world. Sometimes he couldn't help admiring the mind that could pull this off. If It just didn't have to . . .

Sometimes Jamie had a faint hope, that It would be grateful enough for his help not to kill him. He fervently desired to please the Vampire.

Jamie desperately needed It to like him.

It had been Jamie's own idea, checking out the books from the library—there was so much history, current events It had to know. Jamie's ignorance in those matters irritated It unbearably. When It had asked who was president after Washington, and Jamie couldn't answer, he'd been knocked flat—out of sheer frustration.

It read so fast, remembered so well, bluffed so easily. . . . Oh yeah, the Vampire was goddamn brilliant.

Ye Olde Coffee Shoppe, Hawkes Harbor
MAY 1965

BATTERED BODY OF RUNAWAY
FOUND IN BREAKERS AT CLIFFSIDE

Jamie stared at the headline. He put down his coffee on the counter, before the cup shook out of his hand. He and Grenville had seen her briefly the night before, she was trying to thumb a ride. Of course Jamie knew what happened some nights, when the Vampire's pacing increased, when Its speech became disjointed, Its temper erratic—when It could fight the craving no longer and submitted to the foul, humiliating desire—but It had always ranged far afield, not risking any outcries close to home.

The first time Jamie saw It transform into a bat, he fainted.

And last night marked the longest It had been able to keep a check on the beastly longing—maybe it could whip the addiction, Jamie hoped, It so valued self-control. . . .

Jamie dropped the paper like it was on fire, jumped up; fumbling in his pockets for change, he spilled the coins across the floor. Dismayed, Jamie scrambled after them . . . the goddamn Thing counted every penny . . .

A pair of boots stopped near his hand.

Jamie looked up into the cold suspicious stare of Deputy Sheriff Mitch Morgan.

Grenville Hawkes paced the large hall, an ominous sign.

"Why would the authorities question *you?*"

"I toldja when you . . . hired me. I got a bad rep around here. Morgan especially has it in for me. He steps in dog shit he thinks I put it there."

"Stop your sniveling. I'll not stand for it." Its backhanded blow left Jamie sitting, spitting blood.

He cringed when he saw the dark eyes glow red, hastily wiped his face, and looked away. . . . That first time . . . that first time . . .

"Remember, if we're found out, you'll die the same death I will—with a stake through your heart."

"W-w-what? B-but I ain't like you are. . . ." Jamie thought this the one blessing of his life these days.

"You think they'll quibble over details? Not long before my time innocent people were hung as witches. Trust what I tell you. Human nature has not changed, at all."

Jamie went faint, feeling the stake against his breastbone, being hammered through his heart . . .

"Can't you try . . ."

"Try what?" Its head swiveled toward him like a bird of prey's.

"Well, maybe being hypnotized or something? I know a guy that quit smokin' . . ."

Jamie cowered at the Vampire's explosion of wrath.

"You bumbling cretin! I am cursed! Cursed! A curse that can only be raised by the hand that laid it! Mesmerized out of a curse! You fool!"

Jamie had locked eyes with the Thing, he couldn't look away. He was aware of It sticking a poker in the fire, coming toward him with the glowing brand . . . he heard the sizzle . . . oh God, Jamie shut his eyes tight. He waited for the searing pain. He felt a cold finger touch his forehead and collapsed into the corner. Shaking, hugging his knees, he looked up.

Grenville's voice was dry. "If power of suggestion would work, I assure you I could accomplish it. Spare me your idiotic schemes for my salvation. The longer I exist in this form, the more I see the advantages of it. There are terms to my existence, but there are so to others. The unbearable becomes bearable."

It turned and strode out of the room. Jamie looked toward the fireplace. The poker rested in its usual place, cold, untouched. The Vampire had made him envision the whole thing. He could no longer trust his own mind, his own senses. Reality no longer mattered. *It could have made him feel it.*

Darkness came early that time of year. At twilight Grenville would rise from his coffin, still safely hidden in the caves, inspect the work being done on his house—the roof repairs had begun immediately, Jamie choosing the contractor with care—the sight of Grenville easily scaling the sides of the three-story structure never failed to turn Jamie's stomach.

Then they would walk to Hawkes Harbor, Grenville seeing no use of wear and tear on the car, especially since Jamie had failed to clear the road to Its satisfaction. Sometimes they stopped at the Lodge on the land bridge.

It had once been a tourist center, they discovered. A gift shop. There had once been tours of Hawkes Hall, the surrounding woods. Then a tourist disappeared . . . another suffered some kind of stroke, the tours were disbanded . . .

Once again a lodging, it was leased by Dr. Louisa Kahne.

"This must be her," Jamie said. They had paused in front of the town bulletin board. Along with pleas for missing pets, and pleas to take found ones back, BIKE FOR SALE and PTA MEETING, there was a poster for HISTORY OF HAWKES HARBOR—THE TRUTH BEHIND THE MYTH, A LECTURE BY DR. LOUISA KAHNE. FREE. TOWN HALL, JUNE 1, FRIDAY EVENING 7:00.

"At least the price is right," Jamie muttered.

"Truth behind the myth? Ha!" Grenville sneered.

Then Its voice reassumed its deep politeness.

"Good evening, Mrs. Garvey." Grenville tipped Its hat as a townswoman passed by.

"Hello, Mr. Hawkes, Jamie." She smiled as she hurried by.

Jamie's heart stopped for a moment, as it did each time Grenville took notice of a human.

Just as his calluses did him no good against physical pain anymore, his soul had been stripped of all the protective coat he had developed. The thought of this Thing, this monster he had released, harming someone . . . if anyone else had to undergo what he had . . . Jamie had never felt such sympathy for humanity as he did now, when he was exiled from it.

"She's a nice w-w-woman." Jamie swallowed. Shortly after his arrival in Hawkes Harbor, he'd been caught red-handed, stealing tackle from her husband's hardware store. She'd asked Mr. Garvey not to report it, to give the young man another chance. . . .

"Indeed."

"Here." Jamie stopped outside the closed gas station. "See? This is a pop machine. You put in a dime, then you open the door and pull out a Coke or whatever."

Grenville took the offered bottle, and a tentative taste, and hastily handed it back.

"Vile! My God, to drink that instead of ale!"

"Yeah," Jamie said. "I'd rather have ale, too."

"Hello, Jamie!"

Jamie jumped, spilling the Coke. He turned to Katie Roddendem, all speech choked in his throat.

Dressed in rolled-up jeans and a man's white shirt, she still sparkled like sunlight on whitecaps.

"We've missed you at the boardinghouse. The kids want to know when you can visit. Or maybe visit you?"

"No!" Jamie said violently, before he could help himself. Katie blinked and Grenville turned to him with apparent concern. After a moment Grenville said:

"Since Jamie has failed to introduce us, I shall introduce myself. Grenville Hawkes."

"Katherine Roddendem." She smiled, holding out her hand. "It's like seeing a god come down from Mount Olympus, having a real Hawkes visit our village. The rest of your family goes the city."

"Their loss." Grenville took the hand and lightly kissed it. "A European custom. I hope you don't mind."

"Not at all!" She laughed. "That's a first for me."

"The kids can't come to visit," Jamie said abruptly. "There's a lot of work going on. Too dangerous."

"Well," Katie said doubtfully, "come by and see us. Mama misses you. She said so."

"I'm p-pretty busy these days."

"Come now, Jamie, Miss Roddendem will think me a harsh taskmaster. If he is remiss with his visits, Katherine, I shall call with his apologies myself."

Grenville bowed slightly, and Katie laughed as she went on her way.

"What a charming young lady."

"S-s-she's engaged to the deputy sheriff," Jamie said anxiously, as Grenville's eyes followed the girl down the streets.

He didn't seem to hear the remark, and Jamie went dizzy with cold.

Grenville said, "So very full of . . . life."

Katie

"But I don't get it."

"It is not imperative that you 'get it,'" Grenville said. "Follow my orders. That should suffice."

"But why Katie?" If Jamie had thought crawling would do any good, he would have crawled, begged, wept, kissed the black boots Grenville wore. But the only effect that would have would be to enrage the Vampire further.

And Jamie had thought everything might turn out okay, after all. . . . Dr. Kahne had made some progress. Apparently "lifted by the hand that placed it" could have various interpretations. And Jamie would never forget the shock of the evening when Grenville had introduced him to a very old Comoke Indian.

"This is my great-great-great-greatgrandson, Jamie. He will assist Dr. Kahne and me in our labors."

Grenville had seemed as close to happy as Jamie had ever seen It. Maybe that had given Jamie the courage to stammer, "B-b-but I thought W-W-William didn't have any kids."

William, Grenville's son. You think It'd sired Jesus Christ, the way Grenville went on about the guy sometimes. For some inexplicable reason, the mention of William always grated on Jamie's nerves. And since Dr. Kahne's research had shown William had died a hero on the battlefield during the Revolution, Grenville carried on about him even more than ever.

("I never really thought William had the makings of a soldier. I thought him soft, like his mother. It was the worst of him."

"Oh yeah? He's the one that chained you in the coffin, ain't he? How soft is that?"

"I instructed him to stake me."

Jamie was silenced.)

"Martin is my descendant from a different liaison."

The old Indian gave him a toothless grin, and Jamie thought: Fuck. One more person to give me the creeps. Then: So ol' Grenville was messing with an Indian chick. . . . I'd like to know *that* story. . . .

But creepy old Indians were bearable, if it would help with lifting the curse.

But then, it seemed the more progress they made the more nervous Grenville got about it. Like It was changing Its mind about getting uncursed. "Scared" was not a word Jamie could associate with Grenville, but sometimes, you could almost swear . . .

Grenville didn't answer the last question, and Jamie asked again, "Why Katie?"

The Vampire whirled to face him. The eyes were not yet glowing red, yet fierce enough to make Jamie's heart leap, thud against his chest.

"Surely you know," the low growl asked, "that this house is haunted?"

"Hell yeah, I know it's haunted!" Jamie wanted to scream, but only nodded. I'm not that dumb, he thought. There were at least a couple of ghosts, three if you could call that fog of despair by the attic window a spirit. Jamie wanted to put a noose around his neck and jump out every time he passed it.

And whatever clawed and scratched at the cellar walls scared Jamie so badly he'd barely been able to finish the plumbing, ended up doing a shoddy job he was ashamed of.

And one night, when he lay facedown on his bed, wishing he had the strength to cry or the guts to kill himself, he'd felt someone sit on the bed next to him, someone softly stroke his hair, and he was too frightened to look because he knew no one was there. . . .

Grenville said, "Sophia Marie haunts this house. She swore death could not part us, and it has not. If she . . . could inhabit a living body . . ."

Jamie clutched his head. I am going fucking nuts, he thought. This is almost making sense. . . .

"Why Katie?" he whispered. "She's a nice girl. She never did nothing to you."

"There is a slight but definite resemblance to Sophia Marie."

Jamie stared at Grenville. Sophia Marie, his second wife. It had been middle-aged when It had met her; Jamie had always assumed she had been, too.

The Vampire nodded.

"Yes, there was some twenty years difference in our ages." Grenville resumed his pacing. "But never a thought, a feeling, deeper than the width of paper came between us. It was a love few ever experience. . . . When she discovered what . . . I'd become, she offered to share the depths of hell with me, as we had always shared our heaven . . . three times she came to me, begging to become as I was . . . I could not bear the purity of her soul to be threatened . . . when she came to me the third time, I felt myself weakening. I strangled her, rather than have her join me in my shame."

Killed her. To save her. I can't go crazy now. Not yet. I can't let this happen to Katie. . . . Absently, he began to hum. . . .

"But now," Grenville went on, "when I see eternity stretch before me, no one to share my torment, my destiny, I have regrets . . . perhaps we could achieve a semblance of what we once had. . . . She will possess the young woman and I shall make her as I am. . . . She has held true to her word, that she would remain with me . . . death has not parted us."

"Okay," Jamie said. "You bring Katie here, Sophia Marie takes over, you bite her and you guys live sucking blood happily ever after. . . ."

Jamie knew he'd gone too far, but the Vampire was watching him with interest, eyes crinkling, to see how close he'd skirt the edge of danger. It was much more apt to be enraged by cringing than by defiance, though both courted punishments swift and sometimes severe. . . .

Jamie swallowed and went on, "Then what happens to Katie?"

The Vampire held his gaze.

"I don't know."

The tone of voice said plainly, "And I do not care."

"I won't help you." The words stuck in Jamie's throat and died unuttered. Later that night he sobbed them into his pillow, over and over, as if seeking a summons for courage. But no courage came.

Jamie could think of no way to stop It.

Yeah, he wanted to kill It. Lots of times. But if he so much as took a step with that thought in mind, he'd freeze into a cold, shaking sweat.

The Monster not only controlled his will, It had altered the very cells of Jamie's body; biologically, Jamie was programmed to protect the Monster.

If anyone had tried to harm It, especially when It was helpless in the coffin, Jamie would have fought to the death to save It. The thought of It helpless in the coffin provoked an emotion close to pity. And until Louisa Kahne was brought into the secret, Jamie was the only one who knew. Sometimes it felt like he and the Vampire were joined together in some strange brotherhood. . . . It was almost like he cared about It. . . .

"I can't do it." Jamie entered the great hall. He didn't notice he was trembling, it was too common now.

Louisa Kahne glanced up at him from across the huge oak table. To her, he was a small part of a large puzzle—she was curious, but detached. But something in his tone just now caught her attention. For the first time, she thought of what Jamie had to suffer.

"Go to your room," Grenville said. "And we shall have a dis-
cussion about what you can and cannot do."

Hours later, Jamie lay curled up on his bed, weak and nauseous,
his throat throbbing.

I can't do it. Not to Katie. I'm not bringing her here. She's
special.

He remembered the first time he saw her, sassing the other
lodgers in the boardinghouse while she served breakfast. It
seemed years ago, now. A different lifetime. A different life.

A pretty, lively girl with honey-colored hair and deep blue
eyes, something a little crooked in her smile.

She'd poured him a second cup of coffee without asking, returning his brief smile with that infectious laugh, like she knew
he was so hungover he couldn't speak.

He watched her bring people their orders, friendly and com-
petent. She seemed to know everyone.

And everyone seemed to brighten in her presence. It was a
gift, to bring happiness like that.

Jamie'd thought he'd talk to her sometime, when he wasn't
fighting a killer headache, see if maybe she'd go have a drink or
something, he could use a little brightening up.

Then he heard she was engaged to the deputy sheriff, Mitch
Morgan, and scrapped that plan. He didn't need that kind of trouble, he found enough on his own. But still . . . just talking couldn't
hurt. He found himself looking forward to just saying "Hi."

Jamie remembered one of his last conversations with her,
when he was still a free man, when the rumored treasures were
only children's stories.

It was very early one morning, as he sat on the second-floor landing, she passed by on her way to work.

"Hello, Jamie. This is early for you, isn't it?"

The sun was barely casting a pink glow on the sea line.

"Not early. It's still last night," he muttered. The only reason he was sitting there was because the landing was as far as he could go—he'd stumbled on the top step and was unable to get back up, get to his room. His whole body ached, but he had given as good as he got, he thought with satisfaction.

Katie took another look, disappeared, and returned with an ice pack.

"Here."

She sat down beside him, lit a cigarette, while he held the pack to his eye. After a moment she said, "You always seem so angry, Jamie. I wonder why that is?"

"Not angry," he snarled at her, and then grinned at her explosive laugh. Jamie couldn't have stood anyone's laughter at that point, anyone's but hers.

Angry, huh? Well, maybe so. It didn't take much to set him off these days—Kell too focused on the harbor society to give him the time of day—no money, after that big payoff in Boston, a bonus, too, from Greg . . . Stuck in this little backwater dump, he had to go twenty miles north or south to find a decent brawl. . . .

No plans. No dreams. And sick of cons. No energy to ship off. Couldn't even find a decent fight; the locals were truck drivers, mill workers, fishermen who had no concept of the ruthless, vicious violence Jamie had learned in foreign ports. It'd taken three of them to bring him down last night, and Jamie was fighting drunk.

"You're not a bad person, Jamie."

"Not a good one, either."

This was not his usual conversation with a woman, he thought. No banter, heavy on innuendo. No challenges. No threats. Just talk, like you could with a friend . . .

"Well," Katie said, rising, patting his knee lightly, "that's still up to you."

Hawkes Harbor, Delaware
SEPTEMBER 1965

"All right." Mitch Morgan dragged Jamie into the alley between Garvey's Hardware and the post office. He slammed Jamie up against the brick wall.

"What do you know?"

"What do I know about what?"

"Katie's disappeared. And don't tell me you haven't been looking at her, talking to her."

"It's a f-f-free country," Jamie stammered. Oh God, he might have known, Grenville had taken her himself, deciding It didn't need Jamie's help after all; It must have given up the fight against the curse.

Mitch threw him up against the wall again.

"Where is she, you little bastard?!"

"I'm telling you, I don't know! When . . . when did she . . . ?"

"Early this morning. Before dawn. She was fixing breakfast at the boardinghouse, went outside for a smoke. Nobody's seen her since."

"I don't know nuthin' about it," Jamie muttered. But there was guilt on his face and Mitch saw it.

"I'll kill you," Mitch said slowly. "We don't find her safe and sound, I swear to God I'll kill you."

Jamie shrugged out of his grasp, too heartsick to be mad. He looked at Mitch, not seeing a bully needing a lesson but a man terrified for someone he loved.

Mitch, puzzled, turned away. Scowled.

"I mean it, Sommers," he called over his shoulder. "I'll kill you."

If I get lucky, Jamie muttered. He looked up at the sky. It was the only way he could tell time anymore, his life revolved around light and dark.

Getting close to midday. Maybe Sophia Marie hadn't taken over yet; it was likely she'd wait for Grenville.

Jamie wadded up the list of tasks to be done in town, stuffed them in his pocket. Then stopped himself from racing back to the Hall. Maybe he'd be followed. He took his time, picking up the mail. The mailman wouldn't deliver to the island, refused to go nearer than the Lodge, said he never could find Hawkes Hall, though the road was clearly marked.

Jamie idled in the Coffee Shoppe, till he heard the search was centered on the cliffs, by the highway where the other girl was found. . . .

"Katie?" he called loudly, entering the Hall. It was unlikely Grenville had taken her back to the caves, where the coffin was still hidden. As far as Jamie knew, Sophia Marie couldn't leave the house. Not that he knew all that much about ghosts.

He stood in the great hall and listened. He thought he could hear something, like a mewing of a lost kitten. From above— the attic storage room, it had a lock on the door and no windows, contained old pieces of furniture intended for rooms as yet unfinished . . .

Jamie raced up the staircase, ran to the back room where the ladder led to the attic, climbed quickly.

"Katie?" he whispered at the door. He heard the soft sounds again, couldn't quite make out the words. He fumbled, cursing, with the large set of keys, shoved his shoulder into the door—

Aw, geez, Katie . . .

He took a step closer to where she sat, on an antique sofa.

There were dark circles under her blank and mindless eyes. Her skin was gray and greasy, even her hair had gone lank—all the vitality drained from her, leaving a dull and shaken shell.

"God . . ." He'd give his life, he thought, to put her back, unharmed, where he'd first seen her. She didn't deserve this.

She was tearing the edges of her white shirt into a ragged border, whispering as she worked. The childish whimper grew louder as she watched Jamie approach; it grew into an earsplitting shriek.

"What is he? What *is* he? *What is he?*"

He sat with his arms tight around her. She had finally looked up at him long enough to cry, "Jamie," and wrap her arms around his neck. He patted her gently, inspected her throat. Then he just held her, patting her, soothing her while she fought through her hysteria.

It hadn't hurt her bad, Jamie decided. Just nipped her enough to get control. Not much more than scratches. Not that vicious tear It was capable of when ravenous or angry. Jamie cringed, touched his own throat. Of course, It wouldn't want to hurt what was going to belong to Sophia Marie.

Gradually her sobbing stopped, she pulled away. She swallowed.

"What is he?" Her eyes were sane now, her voice was almost calm. "What am I doing here? Jamie—how much do you know?"

An hour later, she knew as much as he did. They sat silent, their fingers intertwined.

"Maybe it won't be so bad," Jamie offered finally. "Being Sophia Marie. At least you'll be alive, sort of."

"I want to live life, not death."

Her other hand patted his, and he tried not to flinch. He'd had nothing but pain from contact, for many weeks now.

"All this time," she said softly, "you've had to live like this."

She was the only person in the world, he thought, who could understand him, could know what his life was like.

And that she could think of him in the midst of her own tragedy made tears come to his eyes.

She leaned her head against his shoulder.

"I wonder what Momma and Trish . . . and Mitch are going to think?"

"That you fell madly in love with Grenville and ran off with him, I guess," Jamie said. It wouldn't be hard for most people to believe—the Vampire was rich and handsome, Jamie had seen the way most women looked at It.

It wouldn't be so hard to believe. Unless you knew Katie.

Katie shuddered violently.

"I guess they'll wonder all their lives. . . ." Her voice trailed off.

Jamie's throat was so tight he couldn't speak.

"Jamie," she said suddenly. "Make love to me."

"W-w-what?" he stammered, drawing back from, searching her eyes.

"Make love to me. Now."

"Katie, don't, come on, don't . . . I told you, I can't let you go."

It killed him, that she'd try even this, she'd be this desperate to escape.

"I know. It's not that—I don't expect—I only have a short time to be alive—I can be alive, Jamie, not much longer! I want to feel all I can, do all I can, be alive all I can. There's so many things I wanted to do! I thought I had the time . . . go back to school, maybe try to write . . . get married, have lots of babies . . . I wanted to ice-skate in downtown New York at Christmas . . . I wanted to know what it was like, making love . . . And now, there's no more time . . . That . . . *thing* is going to . . . I won't let him be the first!"

Her eyes were feverish as she clutched his arm.

"B-b-but Katie, you don't love me."

Jamie knew that was important to nice girls, important that they were loved in return. He never understood why they had to play that game, it was so pathetic, how they didn't seem to real-ize "love" was an easy word from a man with a hard-on. But now, when it was true, he was too scared to speak. . . .

"No, not like I do Mitch . . . ," she was saying, "but in a way, I do—in a way I always have; I've always known you were lonely, Jamie, and somehow, we've been together, now . . . I do love you Jamie, a little. . . ."

"I couldn't. It'd be like raping you or something, taking ad-vantage . . . Katie, I don't want to do wrong stuff anymore, and I'm having a tough time figuring out what's right."

"Jamie, please . . . don't let *him* be my first time. Let *me* get to choose. . . ."

She was unbuttoning her shirt, it hung open, she released, removed her bra.

"Katie, don't—"

Her lips on his stopped his breath. So soft. So gentle . . .

He groaned as his hand slid almost involuntarily inside her shirt, found and caressed her breast, the nipple hardening in his hand. . . .

It had been so long . . . and Jamie hadn't even been sure he'd be able to again, had thought maybe that part of him had died. . . . He'd lived so long with cold and death and darkness . . . Katie was warmth and life and light. . . .

She fit in his arms like she belonged there. Her kiss said more than words. Slowly, he pushed her back down. She drew him to her. He kissed her eyes and cheeks, went back to explore her mouth. . . .

She took in his tongue, gently sucked it. Her hands caressed his back. He had never dreamed such tenderness . . . she did love him, just a little. . . .

He'd always wondered what the girl felt, how it was for them, and it was like Katie was telling him . . . he knew what she was feeling, what should come next . . . he forgot what he'd learned from other women. There was only Katie now. In a way, it was his first time, too . . . he felt alive . . . so much alive. . . .

She gasped when he put his mouth to her breast, removed her jeans, settling between her legs. He couldn't stop kissing her.

Their hearts seemed to beat together, their minds intertwined as well. A comfort, a healing, a sharing . . . alive . . . alive . . . alive. . . .

The welcoming movement her body made as he entered her made him sob aloud.

Katie   Katie   Katie

When they climaxed together, their tears mingled on their faces, Jamie thought his heart would crack.

He lay on top of her, his face buried in her neck. Oh, God he loved her. . . .

Her arms tight around him, she whispered, "I'll never forget you, Jamie, never . . . no matter what."

(And always, when he dreamed of this, and he did as long as he lived, the dream was kind—not till this moment would he awake, her voice still in his ears.)

He rolled over, drew her head to his shoulder. They lay in silence.

He's not going to do this, Jamie thought. I won't let him. He'll have to kill me first.

How strange that he was happy . . . but true . . . here and now he was truly happy. . . .

Katie raised her head.

"Did you hear something?"

"No. You think he's comin'?"

Jamie stood, adjusting his clothes, listened. Usually he felt it, when the Monster left the coffin.

Sometimes It had a job for him right away, commands would flood his brain. Sometimes he was there before the coffin finished opening . . .

"No." Katie stood, looked around. "I just thought I heard a voice . . . a woman's voice."

Jamie whirled around. "Don't listen to her! Get out of here, you goddamn ghost!" he shouted.

He clamped his hands over Katie's ears. The only sound was their harsh breathing. Gradually, he relaxed enough to let go.

"How much . . . longer?"

"'Bout an hour, I think," Jamie answered. He and Katie

wrapped their arms around each other. Their hearts still beat together. Alive Alive Alive

He was resolute. Not this. Not her.

It would have to kill him first.

"That can be arranged."

Grenville stood before them. Katie made a small sobbing sound, frozen where she stood.

Grenville glanced at her, then turned to Jamie.

"I believe you were musing on your death?"

Jamie said, "You can't do this. Not to her. It's not right."

"And how do you propose to stop me?" The Vampire took one step, his cold finger brushed Jamie's head.

Jamie's knees gave out, he rolled helpless on the floor. Grenville turned again to Katie. She still stared, openmouthed, her eyes wild and empty.

"Come, my heart," the low voice beseeched the air. "Come and join me."

"All right!" Jamie shouted as he struggled back up. "You go ahead and do this, kill Katie, I can't stop you. I seen people kill before—for money, God, or country, and you with your 'necessity for existence.' I even did it myself once. But don't you call it love! This isn't love!"

If a dog had suddenly sat up and spoke, Grenville would not be more astonished.

"No, my dear, my dearest love."

It wasn't Katie's voice. A low cool voice, musical and vibrant.

They both turned to the young woman. Jamie shivered. There was a glow to Katie's face, her features indistinct in a shimmering mist, her clothes blurred into a gown.

A low groan escaped Grenville's throat, and Jamie saw tears run down his face.

"Sophia Marie." He took her in his arms, stared down at her, as if he stood on the edge of hell, and she his hope of heaven.

"I am with you, always." She gently placed her hand on the side of his face. For a moment it seemed as if that face would shatter, then he groaned again and nuzzled into the caress.

"Always," he said, his eyes closed.

"But not like this, dearest heart."

He opened his eyes in instant comprehension.

"I cannot bear it," he whispered, holding her nearer.

She pulled back a little, stroked his face as if in wonder. "Ah . . . love."

Their lips met, and Jamie turned away.

The shimmer faded, the glow dissipated . . . the word "always" echoed in the air. Jamie, startled, looked back.

Katie hung limp in the Vampire's arms. The Vampire touched her hair. Once again her eyes were empty. . . .

"Take her and go." Grenville almost tossed the limp body at Jamie. "Both of you, go!"

Jamie found he could use his legs again. He scrambled to his feet, half carried, half dragged Katie with him.

He didn't know how they got out of the house. He ran, dragging Katie by the wrist, looking down at the muddy road just in front of him—scared to look behind, to see if they were being followed, scared to look up, in case It stood before them. It was very fast, when necessary, faster than any human.

Safely across the peninsula, where the town's main street met Hawkes Hall Road, near the marshes and old docks, Katie stumbled, bringing Jamie down with her, his foot twisting under him as he fell. Exhausted, he lay there for a moment, then raised his head.

His heart pounding. Katie's gasping sobs. He listened intently. Nothing else.

No birds. No crickets. No frogs. No sound at all.

He had a strange flash of memory—clear water, white sand, but no bright fish—

He pulled Katie to her feet.

"Go on!"

Her slack face frightened him—had she lost her mind? Jamie remembered the Vampire, touching her hair. He pushed at her, hobbling.

"Run!"

A dark form took shape from the shadows. Katie collapsed to the ground.

"So it was you after all, you little bastard." Mitch Morgan had his rifle to his shoulder.

Holy shit!

Suddenly the dark seemed to be teeming with life, like a kicked anthill.

"Mitch! Don't!" another voice called.

A policeman was bending over Katie.

She's safe. Katie's safe. Jamie turned to run.

The first bullet hit six inches left of his neck, jamming into his collarbone. He staggered but kept on going. Bullet number two cracked a rib, damaged his left lung.

Three shattered his right shoulder blade.

In all, it was twenty seconds between the time the first shot echoed and when Jamie plowed facedown into the mud.

But his mind had long since left. Other than the blows of impact of bullets one and three, he felt no pain at all.

Instead, a sensation akin to the bliss of release.

It's over.

It's over.
It's finally . . .
Over.

Main Street, Hawkes Harbor, Delaware
APRIL 1968

"There's that Jamie Sommers. You know, when I see him staring at you like that I just want to go bust his chops."

"Oh Mitch, don't . . . I really do think he's harmless. Maybe he just found me in the woods, the way he said."

"Harmless, hell, what was he doing that night? And the way he's stalked you since Grenville Hawkes got him out of the nuthouse . . ."

"He hasn't stalked me, he's just tried to be friendly. I'm sure he doesn't mean to frighten me."

"Well, he had something to do with your kidnapping. I'm convinced of it."

"I don't think so. . . ."

"Why? Because you're sorry for him?"

"No, though I am—when I see Jamie, I'm just not frightened . . . I just feel . . . sad."

"Well, I guess every town needs a village lunatic—Hey, let's celebrate getting the loan. How about a picnic Saturday? You can fry up some chicken. . . ."

"Or you can fry up some fish!"

Katie never did remember what had happened while she was missing.

And over the course of years, the course of her rich, full life, it grew of less and less importance. A mystery, but one that didn't seem to matter much anymore.

(Though once, while ice-skating in downtown New York, with her husband and her troop of little boys, there was something in the solemn smile of the smallest as he trudged by her, that made a memory, light as a floating snowflake, brush her mind before melting away forever. Tears jumped to her eyes, though she could not say why—she was so happy.)

Gradually, touched by his quiet devotion, she came to regard Jamie Sommers as one of her dearest friends. Even Mitch finally knew he meant Katie no harm. And made no objection when Katie named their youngest James.

Katie lived life with a fierce enthusiasm, joyed in love, embraced her sorrows, felt every sensation, even tragedy, to the utmost—she might have anyway, it was her nature.

Katie was very lucky. But it was debatable whether she was luckier than Jamie, who treasured his shattered shards of memory.

Who always loved the dream.

Leaving
Terrace View

Terrace View Asylum, Delaware
JANUARY 1968

Dr. McDevitt sighed as he shut his door behind the prospective patient and her mother.

He had become a doctor largely because of his desire to help people—it was hard to admit there were some he would rather refer to others.

Why did they do it? This young lady thought lysergic acid diethylamide would let her see God—whatever she saw, it wasn't God, and she might see it for the rest of her life.

The human mind was as fragile as the human body. Dr. McDevitt felt toward those who deliberately risked it as he would toward someone who jumped off a building to learn what the sensation of falling was like.

The sensation of falling might not last nearly as long as the sensation of hitting the ground.

They want to see God, let them get up and watch the sunrise, he thought.

He would accept her here as a patient but refer her to another doctor—perhaps Dr. Stanley. He was young, building a career, maybe he could understand better why the young people today thought their minds expendable. Dr. McDevitt had to deal with too many of the walking wounded, crippled by the blows of life. Why ingest poison . . . ?

Dr. McDevitt sat for a moment. He had weaned himself from cigarettes two years ago—the medical evidence against smoking was so overwhelming he found it hard to believe it wasn't public yet—but at times like these, the urge was so strong. . . .

Drug addict, he chided himself.

"Dr. McDevitt!" Nurse Whiting came rushing in without her usual knock.

"Did you know Dr. Kahne is here?"

"Louisa? Here? Now?"

Once the shock passed, Dr. McDevitt was glad—he wished she'd given him notice, he could have had an organized agenda for her, but there was so much to discuss. It had been a long time since she'd been there—thanks to her grandfather, she was supposed to be head of the board, yet Dr. McDevitt had to make the decisions.

"Did you know she's releasing Jamie Sommers?"

Dr. McDevitt was jarred out of his listmaking.

"She and Mr. Sommers's employer arrived about an hour ago—they visited Jamie for a few minutes and now she's in the office filling out the release forms."

"You must be mistaken." Dr. McDevitt leaped to his feet. He knew she wasn't. He had long suspected the young nurse of having more than a professional interest in Mr. Sommers.

"I'm not!" she asserted, almost tearfully. "Jamie's in his room, packing, he's so excited . . . it's the first time I've seen him happy."

Dr. McDevitt rushed past her. If this were true—it was pure madness. . . .

He went first to Jamie's room.

Jamie had his battered duffel on his bed and was stuffing it with anything at hand.

He looked up at Dr. McDevitt.

"Grenville came to get me," he said. "He didn't forget. He was just waitin' till I got well—I get to live in the Hall again."

Dr. McDevitt bit his lip. Louisa Kahne had caused this—let her handle it.

There was no way on God's green earth Jamie Sommers was leaving Terrace View. Not in his condition.

"Jamie," he said kindly. "Don't pack all your clothes. If you get to leave, you don't want to be wearing your pajamas."

Jamie didn't catch the word "if."

He looked down at what he was wearing.

"Hey, Doc." He laughed. "Thanks. Don't want to leave in this fuckin' robe. Hell, I gotta start watchin' my mouth. Grenville don't like bad language. Man, I was so surprised to see him. . . ."

"I'm going to go speak to Dr. Kahne. Jamie, do you really want to leave? You never wanted to before."

Jamie stopped, confused.

"Where was I gonna go?"

Louisa Kahne was in the billing office, where the clerk was filling out forms.

"Dr. Kahne," he said. "May I see you a moment?"

He knew now—she'd come to get Jamie Sommers, nothing more. She'd hoped to avoid Dr. McDevitt altogether.

She gave a few quick instructions to the clerk, then went to Dr. McDevitt's office with him.

"What is the meaning of this?" he said abruptly.

Louisa tilted her chin defensively.

"I had an interview with Jamie this afternoon, and—"

"If you so much as said hello to him you know he is in no condition to leave this hospital."

"I will continue to oversee his treatment, on an outpatient basis—"

"*You?* You didn't so much as oversee his transfer from Eastern State—they sent him in a police car, in a straitjacket! You've never even visited the man. How on earth can you oversee treatment for him?"

"You yourself have said in his progress reports that he is making rapid improvement."

"Rapid improvement from a state of near catatonia is not the same as saying he can function outside this hospital! Louisa, what are you thinking? The man is prone to hysteria, paranoia, even occasional hallucinations. He's emotionally a child, as well as mentally unstable. He is not capable of making a trustworthy decision. His short-term memory impaired, his long-term memory very questionable—some days he doesn't even know where he is."

"From what I saw this afternoon, he will be fine in a supervised environment."

"Hawkes Hall?" Dr. McDevitt asked.

He had his suspicions about the benevolent Mr. Hawkes and the stories of the strange Hall gave him the creeps.

"Mr. Hawkes will gladly take responsibility for Jamie. He lives very quietly—Jamie will be subject to no undue stress."

She fiddled with her bone-colored gloves, unable to meet his eyes.

"Mr. Hawkes is anxious to have Jamie back, Jamie obviously wants to go . . ."

"Louisa, if I released every patient who wanted to go home, to every family anxious to have them, there would be no one here tomorrow. You know better than to weigh in that factor."

Louisa said nothing. She still looked down.

"What caused Jamie's breakdown? He was living in this supposedly quiet, nonstressful environment where you must have seen him occasionally—what could have caused a mental collapse that severe? Surely you have an opinion."

"You saw the report—he was shot three times by the police. He came out of the coma into extreme pain—his mind was gone at that point."

"I've talked a great deal with Jamie Sommers—the fact that he'd end up shot by the police doesn't seem to surprise him in the least. He has made remarkable progress, physically, I'll grant you, this is a tough kid. But he'll never be what he once was, physically or otherwise."

"Jamie was always odd, nervous, unstable. Grenville was patient with it because Jamie was trying to reform, because he was very useful. . . . He still believes Jamie innocent of any wrong-doing. . . ."

The way she said "Grenville."

There we have it, Dr. McDevitt thought. She's doing this for Grenville Hawkes. She will run over me, sacrifice Jamie, turn her back on her own ethics, for Grenville Hawkes.

Louisa Kahne, who'd always been above that sort of thing.

"Besides," she continued, "Jamie is an orphan, we have no way of knowing what he might be genetically disposed to."

"I'd stake my reputation this is a trauma-induced psychosis. He has no organic symptoms at all."

Louisa took a determined breath. "Phillip, Jamie is committed here under my orders. I have the authority to release him into my custody. I am going to go finish the paperwork now."

Dr. McDevitt was familiar with that expression—he'd seen in on Dr. Johnas Kahne's face many a time.

You couldn't budge the old goat when he was like that, and his granddaughter was the same.

He felt a stab of despair on Jamie's behalf.

"Louisa . . ."

"Yes?"

"Be kind to him."

"Have I ever been otherwise?"

"Many times, when it suited your purpose. And this is one time more."

She left, and he measured the extent of her guilt by the lack of her anger.

Dr. McDevitt paced his office for a minute. He tried to think of some way to prevent this—other than going to Jamie and pro-voking a bout of full-blown hysteria—easily done, but which his medical ethics could not support—he could think of nothing.

Suddenly, he had a determination to go meet Grenville Hawkes.

He'd heard enough about the man to form some opinions—Jamie had no idea how revealing his comments were.

He went to the visiting lounge. Through the French doors he could see a tall, dark-haired man strolling through the room, flipping a magazine, examining the checkerboard.

He went in.

"Mr. Hawkes?"

The man turned. Handsome, in a commanding, confident way, aristocratic, smooth-mannered.

"Yes?"

It was worse than Dr. McDevitt had even imagined.

This man is cold, he thought, he is dangerous, he has secrets—

"Dr. McDevitt." The doctor held out his hand.

Grenville's handshake was surprisingly warm, and his voice deep and vibrant.

"You have been treating Jamie? I am grateful. Louisa has told me of the progress he's been making."

His dark eyes burned into the doctor's soul.

Dr. McDevitt's profession required a degree of hiding his thoughts, and he hoped Mr. Hawkes would not be aware of how deeply he was repulsed by him.

And I have to turn that—it was ridiculous to think of Jamie Sommers as a child, but it was the first term to spring to mind—confused young man over to this sinister presence. . . .

"I want you to know, Mr. Hawkes, Dr. Kahne is doing this entirely against my recommendation. Jamie Sommers is not ready to be released."

"Is that your opinion? I am sorry. Jamie seemed quite himself to me. A little quieter, perhaps, but then, he was always somewhat reticent . . . and so very happy to be going home."

"A ten-minute conversation is not enough on which to base an opinion—I see Jamie daily and he is a very sick man."

"Dr. Kahne does not agree. And I must support her. Of course, my personal feelings must not interfere in a medical argument, but I will be glad to give Jamie a home again. He was always very useful. And I'm quite fond of him, besides."

This man has come for his dog, Dr. McDevitt thought. Nothing more.

The doctor felt his anger mounting. Between Louisa Kahne and Grenville Hawkes he was helpless. And Jamie was lost.

Neither cared a smidgen for Jamie Sommers. His sanity, his safety, his happiness wouldn't matter a whit to either.

And Louisa must have lost all perception if she didn't realize what kind of man this Hawkes was—

Jamie, with all his criminal background, *was* a child beside him. . . .

"So you won't change your mind?"

Grenville smiled, and it chilled the doctor's heart.

"Surely it's not up to me. Dr. Kahne is making her own decisions."

Like hell, Dr. McDevitt thought. He couldn't rescue Jamie, but he still had something to say to Grenville Hawkes.

He had no business provoking this man. For Jamie's sake, if not his own.

It was a mad, dangerous thing to do . . .

(In fact, five minutes later, Dr. McDevitt was in the pharmacy, gulping down two tranquilizers.)

He anticipated anger, but not the deadly look he received in answer, when he asked slowly:

"Tell me, Mr. Hawkes—what *really* happened to Kellen Quinn?"

Last Scam

---

*Jamie pulled the package of baloney from the ice chest and sat at the
kitchen table. He inspected the loaf of bread for mold—it was spooky,
the way things went bad so fast in this house—took a half-hearted bite
of his sandwich.*

*He hadn't been able to eat his lunch at the Coffee Shoppe, not
with the news he'd heard, but couldn't swallow much now.*

It was too close to sunset.

*The bite felt like a piece of jagged cement in his belly. He tossed
the rest in the trash.*

He looked around the kitchen idly. It still needed a lot of work, but the Vampire was rarely in it, there were other things to do first. Jamie knew he should be lighting the candles in the great hall. If he waited much longer, he'd be shaking so badly he'd waste matches.

And the goddamn Vampire might notice. It noticed everything.

Jamie had seen an antique icebox in Betty's Old Stuff store, he could get block ice at the cannery. Maybe it wouldn't be too newfangled for the Monster. It would work better than the ice chest, look better in the room, too.

He'd just have to pick the right time to ask. . . .

Sighing, he picked up the matchbox. No use dreaming of leaving . . . he'd tried often, early on . . .

Jamie almost jumped out of his skin as he turned the corner into the great hall.

"Kell!"

Kell started, too, then smiled.

"How are you, Jamie?"

"How'd you get in here? The door's locked."

"And when did a locked door ever stop me from gaining entry, lad? Surely your brains haven't totally turned to mush."

"You gotta get outta here!" Jamie's stunned nerves began to hum. "Kell, it's almost sundown!"

"So it is. And the war is over in Troy. You have any other earth-shaking news for me, Jamie?"

"You have to leave!" Jamie ran to look out the window. He tried to gather his thoughts. "I heard the mayor ran you outta town today. They found out you were scammin' Lydia Hawkes."

When he'd heard that piece of news, Jamie had felt more than he had in months—relief, grief, envy so strong—thinking of Kell shipping out, feeling an ocean wind—and a final empty loneliness . . .

"Invited me to leave—quite persuasively."

Kell walked around the room, studying the books on the tall secretary shelves, the weapons on the wall, the mess of wood and shavings from the repairs of the windowsills.

Jamie swallowed. He knew that tone. Kell sizing up a job. And Kellen Quinn on the track of money could be a very dangerous man.

"All right, Jamie, let's not waste time. Where's the money?"

"What money?"

"Oh, come off it, Jamie," Kell said impatiently. "This is me you're talking to. I saw you making a deposit at the bank with my own eyes, a week ago. You never made a transaction in your life, without something sticking to your fingers. You think I haven't known you've been up to something here besides repairman for this Grenville Hawkes? Mr. I'll-never-hold-a-land-job Sommers? It's made me sad, boy, to think of all the deals I've cut you in on, that you'd be holding out on me. Sad, and very angry, Jamie."

"Kell, I don't have any money! He's gonna be here any minute!"

"So what if he is? I haven't been livin' so soft I can't handle that fop of an Orangeman. Now, let's dig out the money box, Jamie, and I'll be on my merry way."

Jamie found himself backing up. He'd always had a hard time, taking a swing at Kell—he had to be very mad or drunk. And now he was only scared. . . .

It slowed his reflexes—Kell swiftly backhanded him, then pulled out his Luger.

"You wouldn't kill me, Kellen." Jamie wiped the blood from his mouth, looked at it, and shuddered.

"Of course not, Jamie, but I will hurt you a bit. Unpleasant thought, but you and I have seen unpleasant before.

"Where is it, Jamie? You know me, lad, I will shoot you. Just a toe to begin with, just to let you know I mean business."

Jamie almost passed out from fear—but Kell had no way of knowing what had been done to him, couldn't realize this was any different from their old roughhousing.

And Kell was perfectly capable of doing what he said, if he thought he smelled money.

"Back in my room," Jamie choked out. There were a few coins set out, Jamie was supposed to broker them tomorrow. Maybe Kell would take them and go—quickly. "I'll get them for you."

"How very kind of you—but I believe I can find the way."

"Kell!" Jamie grabbed at his arm. "Don't! I gotta tell you something. He's a v-v-vampire, Grenville Hawkes—you know, one of the living dead."

Kell looked at Jamie, puzzled and amused.

"I knew you came off the booze too quick and sudden. So you're seein' vampires, lad? Quite original."

"I'm telling you! He's dead! But he walks at night! He's evil, Kell, more dangerous than anything you've seen! And he'll be here any minute!"

"You think you could bullshit me? And with such a cockamamie story as that? Reduced to sniffin' household cleaners, are you, lad?" Kell shook off his clutching hand. "Never mind, Jamie, I'll find them myself."

Kell turned, but his jaunty step halted midstride.

"Good evening, Mr. Hawkes—"

I won't remember this, Jamie thought, flattened against the wall. He should have known what Kell would think, seeing him with money. It was what he would have thought himself—they thought a lot alike, sometimes, he and Kellen. . . .

So that was what it looked like, Jamie thought, detached.

The unholy, perverted mock embrace . . . how fast the Thing could move . . .

The expression of terror, sheer ghastly terror—Jamie must have looked like that.

Jamie slid downward to the floor. He closed his eyes but could still hear the rasping noise. . . . He knew what it felt like, those fangs of icy steel deep in your throat, the frantic grasping at one more breath, just one more . . . please . . . just one . . . the cold draining of your life force, blood . . .

I won't remember this, Jamie thought, whenever I think of Kell—I'll think of the first time he bought me a drink, the time he got me out of jail. . . . He taught me how to judge a jewel, a whiskey, a forgery . . . how to roll a joint . . . what to order in a Bangkok whorehouse, or in a Monte Carlo restaurant . . . Kell, he had a friend or a leverage in every port, often they were the same. . . .

Jamie heard the body hit the floor. It was just a corpse, he'd seen those before, it wasn't Kell . . . that voice still echoed somewhere, that great heart still beat on . . .

"Stake him."

Jamie looked up. The dark and depthless eyes . . . a cold finger brushed his forehead.

"Stake him or he will rise and be as I am."

Jamie crawled robotlike across the floor, gathered his hammer and a board.

No, he'd always remember something else—

The cathouse bar in Singapore. Kell making up verses to "What Can You Do with a Drunken Sailor," each one filthier and funnier than the one before. Jamie and the little Aussie hooker had to hold each other up, they were laughing so hard, the whole place roaring . . .

The deadly duel at poker in Paris, Kell never lost his cool—they'd been rich for a while after, Kellen always shared.

The night in that Liverpool pub—he'd recited most of Macbeth, four in the morning and you could hear a pin drop—Jamie wasn't the only one with nightmares after. . . .

Greeting the Burmese pirates. Like he was inviting them to tea . . .

They'd froze and sweltered, lived high and starved . . . argued over women, money, weather. . . . They had laughed an awful lot. . . . Aw, geez, Kell . . . couldn't you listen to me, just this once . . . ?

He placed the jagged edge of board, somehow knowing where—lifted the hammer high above . . . He must have brought it down. . . . He felt something give, in his head, the first strand of a fraying mind snapping. . . .

No, he'd always think of Kell like he had this noon, when he first heard he was leaving town. . . .

Out to sea somewhere, planning his next caper . . . he'd make other friends, Kell had a gift for that, but would remember Jamie fondly. . . . The shark and pirates would always be his favorite story. . . .

Jamie dropped the blood-soaked hammer. Crawled until he hit the wall . . . His eyes still shut, tears streaming, he hummed the best he could . . . what can you do with a drunken sailor. . . .

Aw, geez, Kell, he thought. Kellen . . .

Garvey's

"These ain't the right candles," Jamie said. He'd opened the box to make sure. He'd gone over his list three times to make sure he had everything right; only on the third time did he think to open one carton of candles.

"Now, Jamie," Mr. Garvey said, "these are exactly the same candles Mr. Hawkes has been using since he moved into Hawkes Hall."

"No, they ain't. They're yellow, see? They gotta be white. All the candles gotta be white."

Jamie showed one to Mr. Garvey. It shook in his hand.

Mr. Garvey paused. He was color-blind himself, he knew he couldn't tell the difference. He checked the carton. SEA SUN. Mr. Hawkes always used SEA CAPS. Jamie was right.

"Well, it looks like they shipped us the wrong order. Can't Mr. Hawkes use these until we can get what he wants?"

He'll have to, Mr. Garvey thought, unless he wants to sit in the dark. It still amazed the whole town that a man with the money Grenville Hawkes obviously had would live in a house with no heat, no electricity, and only partial plumbing.

"He's not going to like this," Jamie said, agitated. "This is going to piss him off. Those candles are supposed to be white. You got any off-white, like ivory ones? He might not mind ivory as much."

"No, we're out of ivory, as well, Jamie. Just tell him the factory made an error. It wasn't your fault, I'm sure he won't blame you," Mr. Garvey soothed. Last week a mistake in the order upset Jamie so badly, Mr. Garvey thought for a minute he was going to sit down on the floor and cry.

"Think so?" Jamie asked worriedly.

"Sure."

Mr. Garvey sometimes wondered what they'd done to poor Jamie, off in those mental hospitals. He'd certainly come back changed.

Mr. Garvey had seen him change once before—when Kellen Quinn and Jamie Sommers first came to Hawkes Harbor, Jamie had been pegged as a thief, a bully, and petty hoodlum. He had caught Jamie trying to steal tackle out of this very store.

Then Kellen Quinn left in a sudden hurry—run out of town

by the mayor, people said—and Jamie, who was by then working for Grenville Hawkes, was a changed man.

Quiet where he'd been boisterous, soft-spoken and polite where he'd been loudmouthed and rude; the story was he was trying to reform, and Grenville Hawkes was giving him that chance.

Still, there was an intense watchfulness to Jamie in those days; quiet though he was, nothing seemed to slip by him. He'd had a nervous edge under the quiet, like a man in a dangerous situation who couldn't afford slipups.

Then came the shooting. Katie Roddendem had been kidnapped. It seemed so clear he was guilty. . . . Most people believed it to this day.

And when Jamie came out of the coma induced by three bullets in his body, he was mad as a hatter, crazy, poor guy, and spent months in one hospital after another.

And now that he'd been released from Terrace View Asylum (there hadn't been enough evidence to charge him with the kidnapping), he was changed again.

Maybe at one of those places they'd clipped his brain with an ice pick or whatever it was they did to crazy people; Jamie, nervous, unstable, sometimes incoherent, seemed unable to think logically anymore. Most people thought Grenville Hawkes was a saint to give him a home again. No matter how handy Jamie was, few people could have put up with him.

"Okay, Jamie, just tell Mr. Hawkes we're sorry and the new order is on the way. You've got everything now."

Jamie looked over the list one more time. "I'm going to have to come back for the shovel. Mr. Hawkes took the car and I'm walkin'. I can't carry these sacks and the shovel, too."

He almost sounded like he was rehearsing his excuse.

"All right, Jamie, it's right here whenever you want it, marked paid for. You seem to go through a lot of shovels up at the Hawkes Hall."

Jamie went white. "W-w-w-we're p-p-puttin' in a garden."

He gathered up his two sacks of supplies and left.

Poor nutcase, thought Mr. Garvey. It wasn't even the right time of year to put in a garden. He, for one, didn't believe Jamie had ever kidnapped anyone.

Out on the street, Jamie glanced toward the bank. Grenville had gone to Baltimore this morning but had said he would stop by the bank on the way home.

It would be nice to have a ride. But there was no sign of the black Mercedes.

But there was Katie . . . she looked so pretty, the way the sunlight caught her hair . . . if she looked this way he'd wave, no, his hands were full . . . he saw that Mitch was with her, they got into his truck. Jamie sighed and turned away.

Jamie saw the first of the kids, the ones on bicycles, and his stomach turned to ice.

He had meant to be well beyond the school before it let out. If only he hadn't counted everything three times over . . . if they'd had the right candles . . .

Jamie took a breath. He'd have to keep going now. If he tried to hide in the Coffee Shoppe until all the kids were gone, he'd be out on the road at twilight.

Of the two dreads, the kids seemed the least horrible. He kept his eyes ahead and kept walking.

Just names, he thought, they just call me names, they don't hurt me, I'll get through it.

"Hey, lookit, it's the looney tune!"

The first call came from a group of boys across the street, fourteen or fifteen years old.

A passing group of girls the same age giggled.

Jamie tried to remember what a little shit he'd been at their age; certainly no better, probably much worse. Anything they did, he'd done.

It was payback time.

The thought didn't keep him from trembling. He tightened his clutch on the sacks.

"Hey, P-P-P-Porky," one mocked his stammer. "When you going back to looney-tune land?"

Jamie just kept walking; once he'd gotten frustrated and stopped to argue with them—they'd surrounded and scared him.

It had been a big mistake to let them see he was scared, but Jamie had no way to summon his old bluffs, no energy left for pretense.

He could still hear them behind him, but they didn't seem to be following. Maybe he was through the worst of it. He bit back tears. Something stung his right shoulder, just missing the blade. Jamie thought, My God, are they shooting at me?

He turned to look just in time to catch the next rock on his forehead—it was a big rock, thrown by a member of the Hawkes Harbor High baseball team and it knocked him unconscious.

"Jamie?" Dr. Scott shone a light into his eyes once more. "Do you know where you are?"

Jamie remained motionless, propped back against the elevated emergency-room bed.

Once he was in the hospital, he had regained consciousness

in five minutes; Dr. Scott suspected nothing more severe than a minor concussion.

But he hadn't spoken or even looked at Dr. Scott or Sheriff Lansky, who was waiting patiently to hear if Jamie could identify his attackers.

But Jamie just stared into space. Once in a while a tremor, like a shudder, went through him.

"You think he's lost it again?" Sheriff Lansky asked. He'd been there after Jamie came out of the coma, a medical miracle, but a mental mess.

The sheriff shifted uneasily. He still felt guilty about the shooting. Jamie had been unarmed, and maybe had been doing nothing worse than trying to help Katie Roddendem. You couldn't blame Mitch, he wasn't thinking straight, but . . .

He should have kept a closer watch on the deputy—there was no need to shoot . . . he'd been so tense, and trigger-happy . . . he should have kicked Mitch off the search team, damn, there had been no need . . .

"I don't know," Dr. Scott said. He looked at the large purple knot on Jamie's forehead. "I hope not. He may just be stunned."

"Good evening." Grenville Hawkes entered the cubicle. "Someone at the bank told me Jamie was here."

He looked at the sheriff, the doctor, and finally at Jamie, who remained expressionless, staring straight ahead.

"How is he?"

"Well, Mr. Hawkes, I think he only has a minor concussion; the X-rays showed no fracture, but he hasn't responded since he regained consciousness."

"Perhaps the shock of the attack—I understand he was attacked by a group of schoolchildren?"

"There's quite a few witnesses," the sheriff said.

"Jamie is high-strung, nervous, perhaps he provoked it?"

It was clear Grenville Hawkes didn't believe for a moment Jamie had done anything, but he was a Hawkes, a regular aristocrat, a gentleman of manners, even more, if possible, than the rest of the Hawkes—

Still, still, the sheriff thought, there was a flickering light in the dark eyes, a dangerous edge in the deep yet cold voice—he'd often thought there was more to Grenville Hawkes than most people realized.

The sheriff cleared his throat and said, "Jamie wasn't provoking the attack, and was doing his best to walk away from it, when he was hit with a large rock."

Grenville looked at Jamie, and his face tightened. Sheriff Lansky was suddenly glad none of the suspected kids were in the room.

"This has happened before?"

"Yeah." The sheriff was surprised Jamie hadn't told Mr. Hawkes. "I've seen it happen before. This is the first time it got rough, though."

"Perhaps you might remind the children that a great many of their parents are employed by a Hawkes enterprise—or should I remind the parents?"

The threat was not even veiled, except in the smooth language. The revived munitions plant was now the largest employer in the area. And Grenville Hawkes was the owner and CEO.

"I'll make sure it doesn't happen again," Sheriff Lansky said.

Grenville went closer to the bed.

"Jamie."

His voice, his most distinctive characteristic, vibrated through the room, and Jamie looked up. He seemed torn between grateful relief and abject terror.

"Do you have your medication with you?"

Silently, Jamie dug around in his jacket pocket and brought out a prescription bottle. Grenville read the label.

"No, not this one. You were supposed to take this with lunch. Did you? Very good. Do you have the other one?"

Jamie did another search, and came up with another bottle.

"'As needed,'" Grenville read. "That means when you need it, Jamie. You could have thought of this yourself."

"Grenville, I'm sorry," Jamie whispered.

The sheriff thought he'd never seen anyone this pitiful—like an abused child still desperate for approval. Though, of course, Mr. Hawkes would never abuse the poor jerk.

Grenville turned to the doctor. "Could I trouble you for a glass of water?"

When the doctor returned with the water, Jamie had already swallowed the pill, but he gulped down the water anyway.

"Mr. Hawkes, I'm sure Jamie will be fine in a few days, but meanwhile he'd better not drive, or be up on ladders, or do anything too strenuous."

"I understand. I'm expecting a visit from Dr. Kahne tomorrow, I'll ask her advice as well."

The doctor and the sheriff avoided looking at each other, each concealing his smirk.

Everyone knew about Dr. Louisa Kahne's "visits" to Grenville Hawkes—they were old enough to cut this coy crap.

"Uh, Mr. Hawkes, your hardware supplies were taken back to Garvey's, if you need them."

"Thank you. Please send the emergency-room bill directly to me."

Grenville nodded to each man.

"Jamie, can you walk?"

"Yeah, sure." Jamie stood up. He wobbled, and Grenville caught him by the arm. They walked out.

On the way, Grenville stopped at a soft-drink machine and put coins in for a Coke.

He couldn't understand how anyone could drink that awful concoction, but it seemed to have a soothing effect on Jamie.

Safely in the car, Jamie didn't bother to stop the tears running down his face.

"You mad at me?" he asked.

"No," Grenville said. "But you need to remember your medications."

"I couldn't think—I didn't know where I was—I thought maybe you sent me back to Terrace View—"

Actually, since he hadn't recognized the doctor, Jamie had been afraid he'd been sent to the other hospital—the one before Terrace View where things had been so horrible . . . he'd been remembering something of that place lately. He'd thought before it was just another nightmare. . . .

And just this week, he had had flashbacks to the infirmary. . . . He'd sat at the kitchen table, clutching his hair, begging his mind, Don't let me remember that, not that, please. . . .

But the images came anyway—lying for days in his own excrement, too weak to turn over alone—he didn't know where he was, why he was there, didn't know his own name and no one would tell him—he'd almost literally died of thirst with water right next to his bed—his wounds opened under rough handling, the blood-soaked bandages dried like glue to his back . . . they'd just ripped them off to change them—he'd fainted then, he thought he would faint now . . .

"Good God, Jamie what are you doing?"

Jamie had looked up at Grenville's horrified face, then at the hunk of hair in his hand, bloody at the roots.

"Tryin' not to remember stuff."

Grenville had given him a long dark look, then said, "Let me know if it works."

"I will be mad at you if you continue this pathetic excusing of yourself," Grenville said now. "If you can't think, perhaps that is a sign you need a pill. Now take your time, compose yourself. Garvey's will be open at least another hour."

"We going to Garvey's?"

"Yes."

"Do I have to get the shovel?"

"Yes."

"But Grenville, you can't fight bad stuff with wrong stuff! It ain't right!"

"I will assume this insane babble is a temporary result of your recent head blow. Not a sign that you need to reside permanently at Terrace View."

Jamie was silent. Another tremor sent his Coke splashing onto his clothes.

Grenville reached over and took the can. Jamie wrapped his arms around himself, curled his toes in an effort to control his shaking. Surely the pill would kick in soon.

Sometimes Jamie wanted desperately to go back to Terrace View. Sometimes he had an awful feeling Grenville had been wrong, he hadn't been well enough to leave. He still thought such crazy things. But if he went back now, when he was needed, no one would ever come for him again. He'd be there the rest of his life. He knew it.

But nothing was like the way he had remembered it at Terrace View. All of Hawkes Harbor, Hawkes Hall—it was like a fun house distortion of the way he remembered it. Even Grenville was different. He could go out in the day now, didn't have to prowl around at night. Mostly he was the same, still stern, commanding, demanding, but maybe a little better since he never hit Jamie anymore, or even threatened him much.

"You don't do that bat stuff anymore, huh?" Jamie said.

"No. As I told you before, my progress toward humanity has lessened other abilities, no matter how temporary it may prove. I am now no more capable of turning into a bat than you are."

"That's good. I used to worry about that, that you'd get stuck that way."

"There was no danger. Maintaining that form is very difficult."

"You know, once a bat flew into Terrace View. I thought it was you come to visit."

"I hope you didn't rush about shouting, 'Hey, look, it's Grenville.' "

"I don't think so, but it wouldn't matter there. One guy thought it was Jesus Christ." Jamie shrugged. "Who knows?"

"Who knows, indeed," Grenville said, but Jamie knew he was no longer paying attention. Grenville had a lot to worry about these days. He wasn't sure he'd accomplished his goal, that the blood thirst might again take over . . .

It seemed to Jamie now it was Grenville's turn to try to re-form, and sometimes he seemed as lost as to how to go about it as Jamie had been. But Jamie was scared all the time, and Grenville often lost patience with him.

Occasionally he still said, "I'll kill you, Jamie," but Jamie didn't think he would. Or at least as often as he used to. But sometimes he did say, "Perhaps you need to return to Terrace View, Jamie."

Sometimes he was angry when he said it, but sometimes he just seemed sad. Once, Jamie overheard Grenville say to Dr. Kahne, "You think I had you release Jamie just to make use of him. That is not entirely the case. Jamie is very much on my conscience. But Louisa, he does sometimes tax my patience to the utmost. If I ever revert, please get him safely out of here."

Jamie knew that meant going back to Terrace View. Funny, neither Grenville nor Dr. Kahne seemed to realize Jamie wouldn't mind going back. For a while.

They were really nice at Terrace View, especially Dr. Mac and Nurse Whiting. Even the orderlies who never got rough unless they had to.

Dr. Mac, well, he'd never talked as much to anyone in his life as he had to that guy. Jamie still had that weird feeling, like he'd known the doc before, somewhere . . . no, it was just another crazy thought. A lot of times he couldn't shut up, even when he knew his time was up, knew the doctor was sneaking glances at his watch—he'd tell the doctor anything, never worry about him telling the cops, and somehow things seemed a lot clearer to Jamie, just by talking . . . but it made him sad, too, the way he'd miss Kellen, after.

And Nurse Whiting; sometimes after one of the really bad days, the ones he spent sobbing in his room, she'd come in at night, lock the door, slip into his bed just to hold him, while he cried himself to sleep.

If it stirred his body to memories, if he became aroused, she'd give him a gentle hand job, with no more to-do than she'd give a back rub. She knew what he needed, as he clutched her, was some respite from the terrible loneliness, the sadness engulfing his soul. . . .

He mustn't tell the doctor, she said, and Jamie never did. He didn't think Dr. Mac would mind, if he knew how much it helped . . . but still he never told him.

But the days were so long there. They felt like years sometimes. What would years feel like? He'd wake up and think: I'm at Terrace View. And the day seemed to roll out like forever to the horizon.

That third-floor landing . . . where you could see the ocean . . . how much time had he spent there, remembering other breakers, different shorelines, warmer seas?

And wondering if Grenville would ever come to get him.

You only left if someone came for you. Jamie had noticed that. That one guy, his wife, his parents, his goddamn dog had come up to get him.

The only person Jamie could think of was Grenville. It was the only thing he had to hope for. He'd never realized before how important that was, to have something to hope for. He started praying every morning, "Grenville, please come and get me," and one day Grenville came. . . .

Jamie looked out the car window. A bearded man was trudging along, carrying a trash sack full of clothes. He was talking to himself, the way Jamie often did, trying to glue a thought onto his mind. But often it didn't work, it'd slip right off, he'd end up staring at a pile of pieces with no idea how they went together, while mouthing empty sounds.

"Can I have some money?"

"Jamie . . ."

"Just this one time?"

Grenville gave him a five-dollar bill and Jamie got out of the car. He stopped the man, handed him the bill and looked him in the eyes.

"I see you, man," he said. The guy looked down, mumbled something, and shuffled on.

"That did little, if any, good," Grenville said when Jamie got back in. He gave Jamie back his Coke.

"I don't care. I know that guy."

"Jamie, it's very unlikely that you know him. He's some sort of vagabond."

"Yeah, I do. He was at Eastern State the same time I was. He was in the army, went to 'Nam. Kept trying to fight the battles. One time it took four orderlies to bring him down."

"I see. Louisa has mentioned they've been trying to close Eastern State. That there were abuses."

Jamie was silent.

"We had you transferred as soon as we could. We had to wait until the charges were dropped. Louisa was quite frantic."

"So what are they doing with the patients? Just dumping them on the road?"

"Very likely most of the ones in your ward were sent on to prison."

"Well, that oughtta make them sane for sure."

Jamie watched the man turn the corner. Probably going to the park. That's where you usually saw those guys.

"Wonder where he's gonna sleep tonight."

"No doubt the sheriff will soon move him on. There are shelters in larger cities, they're better equipped to deal. You know, it's been quite inconvenient, setting up accounts all over town simply because I can no longer trust you with cash money."

"Didn't steal any money," Jamie said. The sheriff move him on? Probably take him out and shoot him. Jamie never saw the sheriff without thinking the man would like to finish what they'd started, that he was sorry Jamie'd lived. . . . One day Jamie'd become convinced the sheriff had wired a bomb into the car. If Jamie turned the key he'd be blown sky-high. He'd walked home, watching over his shoulder. . . . The next day, though, that seemed absurd, just like Grenville said. And he got a parking ticket for leaving the car there overnight. . . . Grenville had been so pissed. . . .

"Giving away what does not belong to you is the same as stealing."

"Didn't feel like stealing. Anyway, people act like they're invisible, these guys. Like they aren't even there."

"Beggars are an unpleasant sight. Many people prefer not to see them."

Jamie thought that over. When he'd first been in the navy, there had been beggars in every port. Americans were known to be generous. At first, it was a kick, handing out loose change. Then it got old. Then annoying. And Jamie didn't remember any beggars at the last ports he'd hit, although there must have been plenty. He no longer saw them.

Jamie got out his pill bottle. "As needed." He uncapped it and took another, finished off his Coke. He was always dry-mouthed these days.

"What'd they do with crazy people in your time?"

"Imprison them, or drive them from town to town. Families locked them in cellars, attics, sent them away."

"Guess things haven't changed much."

"You know what I think of your century's so-called progress."

Jamie could use another Coke but didn't want to ask after just giving away some money. He couldn't afford to get Grenville too mad at him now.

After all, Grenville didn't have to send him back to Terrace View. Jamie knew by now it was expensive; Grenville hated to part with dough. Maybe he'd just fire him. What would happen then? He couldn't hold a land job, he sure couldn't go back to sea.

There wasn't much to salvage from the wreck of Jamie Sommers.

Mental breakdown. That was a good word, breakdown. So many things seemed broken now.

His memory—Grenville often had to tell him five times to do something, lost patience by the third.

Courage, that was cracked, it had all leaked out . . . Jamie thought he could remember being brave, or at least being able to pretend . . . not now.

Whatever it was that had held his tears back all those years, it was shattered. If he felt like crying he just did, he couldn't help it.

And his mind—sometimes he couldn't tell what was real, what he imagined, what he dreamed, it was all mixed up . . .

"I don't hear your voice in my head anymore," Jamie said.

"I was rather hoping you heard no one's voice in your head these days."

"No. No one's there."

Jamie had been counting on that, having Grenville's voice in his head again, telling him what to do. He'd thought when he left Terrace View it wouldn't matter if he couldn't think straight sometimes . . . he'd hear that voice.

And he'd lied to Grenville, at Terrace View. Told him he was well and strong, as good as new. But he wasn't strong. Some of these things he had to do these days, the shoveling, the lifting, the brickwork in the basement, he didn't think he could get through it sometimes, and at night he'd ache all over. . . .

Who'd need him in this condition? Broken? He'd be wandering the streets himself, invisible. Trying to think of somewhere to go, to find something to eat, passing people that he knew but they wouldn't see him . . . Even now, some people looked away when they saw Jamie coming . . . and Jamie didn't blame them . . . there were no mirrors in Hawkes Hall, and Grenville was used to doing without, but sometimes Jamie saw a reflection in a storefront and couldn't believe that slack-faced, frightened creature was Jamie Sommers. . . . Oh God, to be living on the sidewalks scared, with winter coming on. . . .

"Are you feeling better?"

Jamie shook his head. "We going home?"

"No. We're going to Garvey's."

"And I have to get the shovel?"

"Yes."

"But I don't have to do the chanting?"

"No. Louisa and I decided that is too much for you."

Jamie looked at Grenville, blinking back the tears. Twice this man had changed his life. It could happen again. In the twinkling of an eye, like the nuns used to say. In the twinkling of an eye. Jamie was in his power still. And the strange thing was, the only time Jamie felt safe, secure, felt like he was where he belonged, was when he was with Grenville. Surely that was the craziest thing of all. . . .

"Jamie, what on earth are you thinking when you look at me that way? And," Grenville warned, "do not answer, 'Well, nuthin',' in that inane tone of voice."

Jamie, his ready reply cut short, paused.

"Well, you know Dr. McDevitt asked me how I met you and

I told him about that night I left Hawkes Harbor, and met you on the road, your car broke down and all, and you offered me a job when I fixed it, since I had nowhere to go."

"Yes. That's the story we agreed on."

"But when I told him, I really thought it was the truth. Like I remembered it happening that way. But it really wasn't like that, huh?"

"No. It wasn't like that."

"The nightmare, I mean, I used to think it was a nightmare, but it's not, is it? That's the way it really happened?"

"This may surprise you, Jamie, but I remember it as a nightmare, too. But if I let them, regrets could paralyze me."

Something in the calm tone of Grenville's voice comforted Jamie. Okay, so that was the way it happened, it was over, done is done. He sighed and looked out the window.

"Yeah, no use regretting. But remorse—remorse can make you atone."

Grenville looked startled at such an insight from such a source. He had thought along those lines himself. But Jamie went on, oblivious. "I was just thinkin', if I got that all mixed up, the most important thing that ever happened to me, what else? I mean, maybe nuthin' is the way I remember it."

"I'm not like Louisa, Jamie, with her harping on repressed memories. If you have exchanged horrible memories for pleasant ones, consider yourself lucky. If you don't remember all that has happened, perhaps it is for the best. I wish I could do the same."

Jamie rattled his Coke and got out to put the can in a trash basket, got back in the car.

"Are you feeling well enough to go into Garvey's now?"

The pills were kicking in. He felt it first at the back of his neck, like knots were loosening. His mind didn't feel wound up so tight.

"Grenville, I gotta tell you, if we're going to Garvey's—"

"For God's sake, Jamie, you must get the shovel! Let's hear no more about it!"

"No! No, that's not it! It's something bad, but it ain't my fault, I swear, you can ask Mr. Garvey! I-I-"

"What is it?" Grenville looked alert, vigilant. "Tell me!"

"The c-candles. They sent yellow ones. He doesn't have any white—I told it to him right, it's on the order, the factory made the mistake, you ask him!"

"The candles! Do you think I give a damn about the candles now?"

Jamie heard the tone, but not the words. He cowered, here it came . . . he was getting fired for sure. He had his eyes shut tight. He didn't see perplexity, shame, and guilt mix with irritation.

In a different tone, after another minute, Grenville said, "You had it right on the order?"

"Yeah. Just ask Mr. Garvey."

"And you told him this was unacceptable, that it needs to be remedied?"

"Yeah, I said you'd be real pissed, to get it right the next time."

"You handled it correctly. Good job, Jamie. Now can we go?"

"Yeah." Jamie's shoulders were relaxing now, his mind felt calm and distant. Good job. He could think. His headache was receding.

Grenville started the car.

"Grenville, after Garvey's, after I get the shovel, could we stop by St. John's chapel?"

If all the nightmares were really memories . . .

"Jamie, it's getting late."

Jamie looked at the mountains to the west, where the sun-light was fading. He held his pill bottle like a rabbit's foot, in his jacket pocket.

"Won't take long. I just gotta light a candle. Say a prayer for someone's soul."

"Why and for whom do you wish to do this?"

"I don't know," Jamie said. "I can't remember."

Vacation

"Jamie! Wake up!"

Jamie couldn't tell if he was dreaming the voice or hearing it—on the chance he was dreaming he rolled over and pulled the pillow across his head.

It was Dr. Kahne's voice; it was very unlikely she'd be in his room in the middle of the night anyway.

He jumped to a sitting position when he felt a hand on his shoulder—any unexpected touch made his heart race.

"W-w-w-what?"

It *was* Dr. Kahne. She looked angry—Jamie tried to think what he could be guilty of now, but he'd taken an extra pill that night and his mind was foggier than usual.

"It's ten o'clock. Why aren't you up?"

Jamie still couldn't figure out why she was there, except maybe . . .

"What's wrong? Somethin' happen to Grenville?" he asked fearfully.

He remembered now why he'd taken the extra pill— Grenville had gone to the city for a company dinner and was going to spend the night there—Jamie always got scared alone in Hawkes Hall.

It wasn't just the awful things that had happened there that he'd witnessed—it held years of horrible secrets, some over two hundred years old. God knows what had taken place within these walls, on these grounds.

At night, if he were alone, Jamie seemed to hear voices trying to whisper those secrets to him—

"No." Louisa Kahne looked at him impatiently. "Nothing has happened to Grenville. I need your help at the lodge. Why aren't you working?"

Jamie tried to remember. It was true he was usually up at seven.

"Grenville said I could have today off, since I worked Saturday. I can sleep late if I want. Me and . . ."

"I don't care what you were going to do, you're going to help me now. Get dressed. It'll only take a few hours."

"No," Jamie said. When he complained to Grenville that Dr. Kahne was always bullying him, Grenville said, "Louisa was born to bully anyone who'd let her. Stand up to her, Jamie. Show some backbone."

"I don't work for you, I work for Grenville, and he said . . ."

"Jamie." Her voice took on that threatening tone that always made him shiver. "You *are* going to help me today."

He knew what was coming next, and grabbed one of the pill bottles off his nightstand, popped three tablets in his mouth, and took a long swallow from his water glass. He'd need all the help he could get to stand up to her.

"If you want to go back to Terrace View Asylum it can be arranged." She brought out her favorite tactic. "So just get dressed."

She turned and left the room. Jamie sat there a moment, thinking it was easiest just to do what she said, as usual. Then he thought, Grenville said I could have today off. He said to stand up to her, I got stuff I want to do today.

He got up and followed her halfway down the hall. She turned and looked at him, surprised to see him still barefoot, still in the worn gray sweatsuit that served as pajamas.

"I told ya before, Dr. Kahne, some days Terrace View looks pretty damn good to me. It's peaceful, at least."

Jamie quailed inwardly to see Louisa's eyes slant dangerously, her jaw jut out. He grabbed onto the stair banister, strangely dizzy all of a sudden.

"And I have told you, Jamie, if I decide to send you back to Terrace View, I'll make sure you spend the rest of your life there."

She spoke almost by rote, this quarrel a familiar rite.

"What are you going to do? Pick me up and put me in the car?" Jamie's tongue felt numb. He had some fuzzy thought of just sitting on the stairs. She couldn't physically put him in the car and drive him to Terrace View.

His knees gave out and he did sit down.

"A forcible commitment order can be easily obtained. In which case I can call the police."

Jamie struggled with a rapidly fogging mind. Was she saying she'd have the police shoot him? Could they just walk in the front door of Hawkes Hall and start firing? Maybe he'd get lucky this time. Maybe they'd shoot him dead. He wouldn't have to go through all the pain, the rehab, the mental hospitals.

The crazy time.

He felt like he was going crazy again, the way he couldn't think. Tears welled up in his eyes. He wished Grenville was here. He'd protect him.

Jamie stared at Dr. Kahne, no longer able to hear her ranting.

He was still coherent enough to know something was wrong. What was it? He shouldn't feel like this. He should feel calm, detached, far away, like he was watching a play. Not like every muscle was dissolving into liquid, that soon he'd be just a puddle of flesh on the stairs.

It shouldn't be such work to breathe. . . . He leaned his head against the vertical railings in the banister.

"Louisa!"

Both Jamie and Louisa started to see Grenville standing in the hallway. He'd come in through the back door and now took three angry strides to stand next to them.

"I told Jamie he could have the day off."

"Grenville, I only need him for a few hours. Surely, it wouldn't hurt—" Louisa wheedled.

"I have told you before, Jamie is mi—my servant and you are to leave him to me. It does no good to frighten him into imbecility."

Jamie could tell Grenville was mad, but couldn't decide if that anger was directed at him or Louisa.

He reached through the railing and tugged at Grenville's sleeve with the little strength he had left.

"Don't interrupt, Jamie," Grenville said impatiently. "I'm speaking with Louisa."

"Grenville, I think I'm dyin'," Jamie whispered.

"What do you mean?" Grenville turned to actually look at him for the first time that morning.

Jamie's face was white, his eyes dilated.

Louisa suddenly actually saw him, too. Quickly, she stepped up to feel his forehead, took his wrist to find his pulse.

"Grenville, he's like ice! And his heart rate's dropping. Jamie, what's wrong?"

"Wrong pills." Jamie's voice was barely audible. He closed his eyes, exhausted from the effort of trying to keep them open.

"Get him into the car." Louisa suddenly took charge again, crisp and commanding. "We have to get him to the hospital. Quickly, I'll be there in a minute, I want to check his pills. I don't remember any medications that could do this."

Grenville pulled Jamie's arm across his shoulders, hauled him to his feet. He had a moment of chill surprise—surely Jamie should weigh more than this . . .

Grenville barely had Jamie shoved into the backseat, had the key into the ignition, was fumbling with his seatbelt, when Louisa leaped into the car.

"Oh, dear God, hurry!" she said, and the terror in her voice made Grenville's pulse jump. "It's muscle relaxants on top of tranquilizers."

They could hear him breathing in deep, heavy sighs, with long pauses in between.

"Please!" she said. "Please hurry!"

Grenville jerked the car into gear, and for the first time since he'd learned to drive, stamped down hard upon the gas.

Grenville sat in one of the sofas in his great hall, fingers together, lost in thought.

He rose to his feet when Louisa came in, as he would for any woman.

That was one of the first things she had loved about him, Louisa thought, the courtesy over courage, like satin over steel . . . she shook her head.

"Honestly, Grenville, you should have a phone installed."

He ignored that remark. "You had a talk with Dr. McDevitt?"

"Yes. He said . . ." Louisa broke off as someone knocked on the front door.

Grenville frowned. "I'm not expecting . . ."

But Louisa, always one to take action, was already in the entry, had already swung open the door.

"Rick?" Grenville greeted his young nephew. "What can I do for you?"

"Here's your mail. I found the new mailman wandering in the woods."

Rick looked around.

"Is Jamie here?"

"Jamie?"

"Yes, he was supposed to meet me and Trisha at the wharf over an hour ago, to give us another sailing lesson. We were going to do it today because he had to work Saturday. I know he sometimes forgets things. . . ."

Grenville and Louisa looked at each other. Grenville spoke. "Jamie is in the hospital, Rick."

"What's wrong?"

"Nothing serious. He got some of his medications mixed up. They pumped his stomach, the hospital assured us he could go home this evening. Right now he's sleeping."

"Great." Rick slumped with relief. "Could you tell him we'll do it whenever he feels up to it?"

"Yes, Rick, I'll tell him. It's nice of you to let him sail your boat."

Rick looked at his older relative with the sudden, hot irritation of the teenager. "I'm not being nice. You sound like Father. Jamie's teaching me to sail and he's going to teach me to drive. He's the one being nice. It's more than Father would do."

"I see. Well, I'll be sure and give him your message."

When the teenager slammed the door behind him, Louisa and Grenville looked at each other guiltily. Grenville remembered—Jamie had taught *him* to drive, too.

"He did have plans for today," Louisa said finally.

Grenville tried to place blame.

"I don't think it's constructive to constantly threaten him with Terrace View. Especially since you know you'd never do it."

"Jamie knows that." For the first time, Louisa was a little uncertain of this statement. "Besides, you threaten to kill him. Surely that's worse."

"He knows I don't mean it."

"Don't be too sure of that—what you said this morning— 'Jamie is mine.' You own him. That's what he believes."

Louisa could not forget Grenville's slip of the tongue this

morning. Jamie is mi—She'd had such an insight into their strange relationship.

Jamie is mine.

Grenville believed it. Of course, he'd owned slaves before. Indentured poor, exiled convicts.

But Jamie believed it, too.

Louisa had much more experience with vampires, vampire's slaves, than did the average layman, knew much more than most researchers . . . She had a classic example in front of her eyes. It puzzled her still.

Even though Grenville was now completely human, even though his strange, almost total power over Jamie was supposedly gone, both men still seemed held by the blood covenant that bound them from the first. She still witnessed examples of what had to be telepathic communication between them.

It could be nothing else. For never, she thought, had two such different men walked the earth. . . .

"What did Dr. McDevitt have to say? Did he confirm the prescriptions?"

Grenville knew well enough what a man under the influence of an uncontrollable urge could do.

"Yes, they're legitimate prescriptions. I received my usual lecture about how I'd had no business releasing Jamie, and this time he added how I could have ever overlooked the list of medications he'd given me at the time. He never dreamed the doctor here would prescribe anything else. He never checked on the re-fills because he assumed I was doing that."

"After all," Phillip had said with uncharacteristic sarcasm, "*You* are his doctor."

"And Jamie is welcome back at any time."

"Should he go back?" Grenville asked uncertainly.

Louisa didn't seem to hear him. "Grenville, I did have him overmedicated, sometimes it was just the easiest thing to do—things were so desperate, and Jamie so nervous, but I promise, I never, ever dreamed he was still using prescriptions from Terrace View, too."

She tried a little fake laugh. "It's no wonder he's been such a imbecile, it's a wonder he's been functioning at all. . . . Phillip asked me . . ."

"Yes?"

"If I were certain it was accidental."

"That's absurd."

"Is it? Freud said there are no accidents. . . . You know, Jamie was put on suicide watch twice at Terrace View."

After a moment Grenville said, "No. I didn't know that."

"Some of these things, the pain relievers, the muscle relaxants, and nowadays they're even suspecting Valium—they're highly addictive. I'll have to start gradually cutting him back. He's going to be terribly anxious."

She paused. "Today—another fifteen minutes and he'd be dead."

Grenville sighed. He rarely gave Jamie a thought. Jamie had been the first person Grenville met in this century—if you could call that violent horror in the cave a meeting—since then, Jamie seemed part and parcel of Hawkes Hall, he was viewed as an extension of Grenville as much as the black Mercedes. So many, so much more important things had gone on in Hawkes Harbor—the removal of the curse, which had exposed a deeper evil still. Then the family, the businesses—God knows what would have happened to either of them, had not Grenville been there to step in, with money and advice.

Jamie and his problems often seemed more of an irritation

than anything else. Yet he had been a good and loyal servant. Even years ago, Grenville had been surprised at how much he'd missed him, during the months of his hospitalization. And today, when he'd feared for Jamie's life . . .

"You told me Terrace View now has a rehab wing, for the sudden increase in drug addiction."

"I can't send him to Terrace View now. He'd think he was being punished. And he would think you were going to abandon him there."

Louisa didn't add she was sure Dr. McDevitt would make sure Jamie was never released to her custody again—he was head of the board now, she wouldn't put it past him. Phillip was up to something at Terrace View . . . there had been maneuvers with the stockholders . . .

"If we could find a relatively stress-free environment for him, away from Hawkes Harbor, just for a while, where he wouldn't have to deal with all the memories here, it might be easier for him to cope with weaning off some of these drugs."

"Can't we just send him somewhere?"

"You know very well he couldn't bear to leave you even if you found somewhere to send him. He will have to be supervised for a while, and you're the only one who could control him. Jamie is yours, remember. I am to leave him to you."

Grenville regarded her with imperceptible amusement. She constantly wavered in attitude toward Jamie, depending on her needs; he was a friend, a slave—or their mutual child. Finally he said, "Surely, Louisa, you are not suggesting I take Jamie to Disneyland."

Louisa had a strong urge to take Grenville by the ears and shake him.

"Of course not."

"Why do you suppose Jamie remains so devoted to me? I assumed that would end when the curse was lifted."

"There is a psychological disorder known as the Stockholm syndrome. Hostages have been known to identify so strongly with their captors that they defend them. You're his only security. Jamie knows very well he's no longer able to deal with that chaos he called a life."

Grenville sat silent for a few minutes.

"Richard was saying . . ." she began. His look warned her he had little interest in what his cousin had to say, but she went on. "The Collins shipping industry needed to look into passenger cruises. They are the wave of the future—you know Roger and his puns."

"No," Grenville said. "No."

"Of course he offered to go. But you could investigate for yourself. And it's not unusual for a man of your position and background to travel with a valet.

"Jamie might be weaned off the medication easier," Louisa said, examining her nails. "And he's very fond of sailing."

"No," Grenville said. "No, Louisa. No."

Grenville was at the hospital that evening at six. The doctors said Jamie would awake about then; if the tests were fine, if no liver damage threatened, he could go home.

Grenville didn't want Jamie to wake up alone in a hospital room; God knew what nightmare he'd make of it.

Jamie was starting to move slightly, mumbling in his sleep. Another bad dream, Grenville thought. Poor Jamie had so many. He still woke screaming a few times a month. If Grenville was still up, and he often was, still not used to wasting the beautiful night hours in sleep, he sometimes went in to Jamie's room and spoke quietly to him for a minute. He couldn't decide if it was touching or pathetic how the sound of his voice comforted Jamie, how swiftly he would go back to sleep.

Grenville could sympathize, having had decades of bad dreams. Being chained in a coffin it gave you bad dreams. Then to wake to a still more horrible reality—cursed, his family long dead, Sophia Marie gone, his son, unable to use the wooden stake as promised, locking him into the coffin for eternity—and always the terrible hunger, the thirst like the most powerful pain. Slowly rage had buried every other emotion, like the strongest fledgling destroying its nest mates.

The injustice of it—other men had done so much worse at much less cost. So he reasoned then. A few words spoken in a heated moment to a native serving girl—surely they were taught, he thought, not to believe what gentlemen might say of love—how was he to know the powers her tribe possessed? He had not realized he had asked her for love, until he murdered it and saw it swiftly decay into hatred.

Grenville thought differently now. It did not matter what other men had done and had not paid for. Each case was judged alone and separate, he believed. No matter what had gone on before, what others did after and escaped unscathed . . . and surely, to invite love, and then betray it was a mortal wrong . . . it was his own hand that laid the curse . . . his own doing . . .

His thoughts went back to the night of his and Jamie's meeting. He had been almost a pure flame of hatred, that night he'd heard the ancient chains being broken, the lid opening. . . .

How had he ever kept from killing Jamie? It was a source of wonder still.

He'd had just enough self-control to avoid a death—he'd found the jugular vein and, ravenous as he was, he was able to refrain from a kill. He knew that centuries had passed, he'd need a guide in a strange new world. And then; the quality of the blood was ghastly—tobacco, alcohol, a bitter narcotic tang; once the edge was off his hunger he was disgusted.

Surely some of his rage those early nights was partly intoxication. The shock of finding out what year it was . . . and, finding the tools, next to his self-made coffin, the slow dawning of what the young man had intended . . .

Even at this late date, Grenville could feel a swift surge of anger. Jamie had felt his wrath that night, and for many nights after . . . it was as if he'd been to blame, somehow . . . the vile young wharf rat . . . who'd set the Monster free. Surely everything between them since had been tainted by that meeting.

On Jamie's side by terror, on Grenville's by contempt.

He remembered Sophia Marie, whose very shade had risen to reproach him. Not for being as he was, God knew it was no choice of his, but for embracing it, taking consolation in his powers . . .

Jamie shifted in the hospital bed, whimpering. Grenville leaned forward, ready to reassure him.

"Kellen?" Jamie called fretfully. "Kell?"

Grenville took a swift breath, and then stared at Jamie with an incurious surprise. Never, in all these years, did he dream Jamie Sommers had the power to hurt him.

"You win, Louisa," Grenville said. "If we stay cooped up in the Hall much longer I'll strangle him."

As irritating as Jamie could be before, now that Louisa had started cutting back on his medications, he was insufferable.

"He's cowering from his own shadow, jumpy as a cat, and if I so much as raise my voice to him, he starts crying. He has more energy than he's ever had, but he can't focus. As far as any work goes, he's absolutely useless."

Louisa sighed. "I think that not having access to all the drugs he thinks he needs makes him as nervous as the actual withdrawal."

She winced away from the memory of telling Jamie she was taking him off some of his medications, how he'd begged her not to, crying like a baby, finally even offering to live at Terrace View for the rest of his life.

Grenville, she remembered, had been careful to avoid *that* scene.

And now, Jamie was in a constant state of nervous anxiety, thinking he needed a pill whether he did nor not, as well as feeling the hellish effects of the actual physical withdrawal.

Grenville didn't have the disposition to cope with the young man's fears; Jamie knew this and it only made things worse. The last thing he needed, and Grenville admitted it, was Grenville leaving him. He would see it as desertion. It could easily cost him what was left of his sanity.

"He'll never be the same again, will he, Louisa?"

"The same?"

"I forgot, you didn't know Jamie very well or for very long before—when he first began . . . working for me he was different. Quite resourceful. Almost clever in a way. And bold enough to risk . . ."

Grenville's voice trailed off.

"No," Louisa said. "He'll never be the same."

They remained quiet for a moment.

Louisa decided to take advantage of this moment of guilt.

"Well, ten days will be long enough to lose another drug—I'll send him with a limited supply. Maybe Jamie will be distracted enough to cope with it."

"And if he's not?"

"I'll send some strong sedatives with you. If he gets too bad you can just knock him out for the rest of the trip."

Grenville looked grim—hardly like a man facing a dream vacation. "This had better work, Louisa. Of all your little plots and schemes, this one had better work."

New Orleans
AUGUST 1968

"Wow, I bet the crew quarters ain't like this." Jamie looked around the spacious first-class cabin. He had never seen a cabin this large on a boat, not even on the yacht on the Riviera where he'd worked as a deckhand.

"Got a private balcony and everything."

Grenville sighed. As spacious as the room was—and he had specified the largest he could get—it was still much closer quarters than the rambling Hall. He tried to imagine living here with Jamie for ten days, then dismissed the thought as unbearable.

At least Jamie was distracted from his fears. If anything, he was too distracted; it would take him hours to unpack if he remained this hyperactive.

Jamie ran back in from inspecting the small adjoining room; for children—or servants.

"I wonder what the engine room looks like. You think we could see it? I never been on a ship like this, some of the freighters were this big, but not with all these fancy decks and everything."

"Remember we're researching passenger cruises for Hawkes Enterprises—go anywhere you wish." Grenville entertained a pleasant fantasy of Jamie roaming the engine room the whole voyage. "Maybe you could investigate how things are run and report back to me."

"Sure, if it's legal and everything. I don't want to get into trouble or nuthin'."

"You won't." Grenville did plan to write up a few notes, use the trip as a tax write-off. "Once you get everything put away, feel free to go anywhere you wish."

"Okay." Jamie wrung his hands together. "Uh, Grenville? There's sure a lot of people here. You think I could have . . . ?"

"No. You can have a tranquilizer at twilight, another one when you go to bed. That's all."

And, Grenville thought, we're supposed to drop one of those before this is over.

Jamie was too excited to go into a sulk. "Okay. Man, it feels so good to be on a ship again."

That's right, Grenville thought. Jamie'd been some sort of sea tramp before they'd—met.

He often forgot Jamie had had any life before.

Well, at least he wasn't cowering around in that disgusting way.

Grenville decided to explore the ship. One this size was new and amazing to him, too. It would be his first sea voyage in this century, he thought.

The idea excited him, and he was able to forget all about Jamie.

"I know these drills are a pain, but if you have to get off the boat in a hurry it really helps."

"Indeed." Grenville felt ridiculous in his life vest. The fact that the other first-class passengers were standing around, chatting, looking uncomfortable in life vests, helped a little.

"Yeah, I had to get off a little cargo ship once—engines caught fire—if the captain hadn't drilled us, we would have been in trouble. It sank fast."

"How interesting," Grenville said, hoping Jamie would shut up. An unpleasant side effect of Jamie's withdrawal was a tendency to chatter.

"Yeah, that time we had to get off a ferry—that was a mess. If you didn't drown the fuckin' crocodiles got you. . . ."

Grenville's attention was caught by a most lovely young lady, who was standing with two elderly people, obviously her parents.

What an intelligent-looking woman, he thought.

"I think they lost about fifty people on that one—it was way overcrowded. I grabbed two kids, but their parents didn't make it . . ."

Grenville walked over to the young woman.

"Pardon me . . ." he began.

"Geez, do we have to dress up for dinner every night?" Jamie pulled uncomfortably at his tie.

"If you want to eat in this restaurant you do."

Grenville had been thinking how pleasant it was to have

Jamie looking like a gentleman for a change, instead of the young thug he was too apt to appear as.

If Leslie happened by, he wouldn't be ashamed to be seen with him. In fact, dressed in his dark gray suit, Jamie might even be called handsome—Louisa often said he would be, had he a different demeanor.

"So, there's different restaurants?"

"Yes, several."

"And you don't need ties in all of them?"

"I understand some are quite casual."

"And we can eat in any of them?"

"For what I'm paying, we can eat in every one of them."

"Well, if you don't mind, this'll be the last time here for me. I know you like this stuff, but I can't eat while I'm bein' choked."

Grenville inwardly rejoiced, but said quite calmly, "I don't mind at all."

Jamie was behaving very well, so far—he'd needed his tranquilizer at dusk, but Grenville had expected that—and understood it, as well.

"I'm going to a poker game this evening," Jamie said conversationally.

"In the casino?"

"They got a casino?"

"Where have you been all day?"

"Engine room. Crew quarters. Nice guys. You better tell Richard, though, it's all union. No getting around it."

"I'll let him know."

"So. You got anything for me to do tomorrow? Does it matter what time I get back to the cabin?"

"No. In fact, Jamie, except for your research project, just treat this as a vacation for you, too. Set your own hours."

"Yeah? Great. Thanks. Uh, would you mind leaving a pill out for me? I mean, in case you're asleep when I get in?"

"Sounds like a good idea. Jamie, don't forget, you're a first-class passenger, too—take advantage of it. You can go anywhere on the ship, any deck."

Grenville couldn't see Jamie taking ballroom-dancing lessons, attending the lectures, visiting the quite adequate library—all activities he was planning with Leslie.

The last thing he needed was Jamie trailing after him.

"Okay," Jamie said. "I will."

The second night Jamie discovered he could have his drinks in the bars charged to their cabin. He'd lost most of his money in the poker game—he hadn't played in years and hadn't been all that good then—not like Kellen was.

Anyway, the crew was a little uncomfortable with him, he could tell, especially after learning he was traveling first class.

He didn't blame them.

But this first-class stuff was all right, he decided, if they picked up your bar tab. Until then he hadn't much liked it—the first-class passengers were either old or stuffy or both. He didn't hate rich people anymore, after knowing the Hawkeses, but he didn't want to hang out with them, either.

Funny, he rarely thought of Grenville as rich. Probably because he was so damn tight. And Hawkes Hall, big as it was, was one of the most primitive places Jamie had ever lived.

There was loud music coming from somewhere—it was a bar patterned on a disco. Jamie was glad to see people closer to his own age going in and out.

He walked in, squeezing by the lively dance floor, to the bar.

Immediately he spotted two girls standing at the bar, ignoring two college-age guys who were eyeing them.

Jamie hated playing games. He moved to the bar, next to the girls.

"Can I buy you young ladies a drink?"

They were about college age, too, one chubby-cheeked and apricot-colored like a chipmunk, the other had cat-green eyes under a tangle of dark curls.

"A banana daiquiri," said the cat-eyed one, with a smile.

"And how about you?" Jamie asked the other.

"Oh, I'll sip hers." She smiled, too, bright-eyed and cheery. "We like to share."

They were both cute, rather than beautiful, but very, *very* cute.

"Really?" Jamie said. "That's interesting."

He noted, with satisfaction, the college boys' ire. When Jamie gave his cabin number, signed the tab, the girls looked at him again.

"That's first class, isn't it? Are you rich?"

"Naw." Jamie sipped his scotch. He never got scotch at home. In fact, he never got alcohol.

"My boss is. I'm travelin' with him. We're researching cruise ships."

The girls seemed unusually pleased with that answer, instead of disappointed like Jamie half expected.

"That is so honest. Usually these ships are full of bullshit artists. I'm Diane."

The dark-haired one shook his hand.

"I'm Michelle." The other kissed Jamie's cheek.

"Jamie Sommers."

Jamie watched, from the corner of his eye, the college boys move on to another group of girls. He gloated.

"We hate bullshitters," Diane said.

"We're very honest," said Michelle.

Jamie could tell, from the way they almost finished each other's sentences, that they'd been friends for a long time.

"So, you girls been on cruises before? What do you do for fun?"

Grenville woke; he'd had champagne at dinner, Leslie wanted a few small glasses, champagne always gave him fitful sleep, he hardly remembered why anymore.

He looked at the bedside clock. Four in the morning. Jamie still hadn't returned, his tranquilizer lay unused on the nightstand.

For a minute, Grenville debated whether or not to worry, then decided not.

With all his vaunted seamanship, it was unlikely he had fallen overboard. If he didn't miss his medication he was probably sane enough.

Grenville was glad that instead of feeling cooped up with Jamie, he actually saw less of him than at Hawkes Hall.

And Leslie—a real lady, her ex-husband must have been a cad, she bore the strain of the recent divorce so gracefully— Grenville drifted back into sleep.

The bunks in third class weren't roomy at all, not much room for two, a real crowd for three, but Jamie and the girls slept as peacefully as pups in a litter.

Jamie had overcome one great hurdle, though not intentionally. Stripping naturally for bed, he'd completely forgotten about his scarred back, until Michelle gasped, "Oh, what happened to you?"

Jamie froze for a second. He didn't want to tell them he'd been shot by the police—there were people in Hawkes Harbor who had been frightened of him ever since, though Jamie thought it would be more logical to be frightened of the cops.

After all, he had been saving Katie, not hurting her.

"Were you in Vietnam?" Diane asked, looking closer.

Jamie thought of the men he'd known in hospitals who had been to war. It would be sacrilege to claim their pain.

"A bank robbery." Jamie had drunk enough not to stammer, which he usually did when he lied. "In Jersey. I was in the wrong place at the wrong time. The guy went nuts and started shooting. It was years ago."

He hated lying to the girls, with their disdain of bullshit, but he was not going over the whole Katie Roddendem thing again.

"I remember reading about that," Diane said. "Wow. How many times were you hit?"

She was naked herself by now, sitting next to him, caressing his back lightly, feeling the scars left by the bullets, by surgery.

"Three times," Jamie said shortly. He took a breath, determined not to cry at their kindness. It was the first time since the shooting anyone other than a doctor had seen his back.

On his rare and strangely listless trips to one of the Ocean City whorehouses he hadn't thought it necessary to remove his shirt.

Michelle sat on his lap. Her lips were soft against his, her hands played with his hair. She was all gentle curves. He ran his hand over her lightly. She traced his lips with one finger.

"You have the most incredibly beautiful mouth."

Jamie slid an arm around her waist, rolling back on the bunk, bringing her on top of him.

"Yeah? Thanks," he muttered. "I like yours, too."

"Make room," Diane said. They moved over.

There was enough room after all.

Jamie woke when Diane slipped out of his arms. He'd been sleeping on his side, the three of them huddled together spoon fashion. Her hair in his face smelled of baby shampoo.

"First dibs on the shower," Diane called.

Jamie felt Michelle snuggle closer, her arm tighten around him.

"She's an early bird," she said. "I'm not in any hurry."

Then she said, "Your poor back."

Her lips softly kissed the scars on his shoulder blade; he felt her tongue lightly caress him. Gently, tenderly, she acknowledged each old wound.

Jamie felt the tears running down his face. No one had ever expressed sympathy for his pain.

He shivered when he felt her lips move to the back of his neck, felt her take his ear lobe into her mouth and suck it gently.

"Turn over," she whispered.

He didn't know how much later it was when he opened his eyes. It was like returning to consciousness.

Diane was toweling off in the middle of the small cabin.

"My turn next!" she stated.

"It'll have to be later," Jamie said honestly.

"Okay. But remember, it's my turn."

After lunch, and two Bloody Marys, Jamie and Diane lay on a single lounge chair next to the pool.

Michelle had gone to a makeup demonstration.

"Is it my turn yet?" Diane whispered to him. "I bet I'm better than Michelle."

"I don't know, she's awfully good."

"I'll prove it. Let's go back."

Diane was better, she used more tongue, but Jamie diplomatically declared it a tie.

Then fell asleep and slept through the twilight.

"Hey, Grenville!"

Jamie was waving at him from the side of the dance floor.

Grenville felt annoyed for a moment. He and Leslie were in the middle of a waltz, one of his favorite dances, Jamie was dressed in the atrocious fashion most of the young people on this boat adopted—cutoff jeans and a souvenir T-shirt—and he'd have to be introduced.

You would think Jamie would have learned some taste after all these years . . .

Grenville gracefully danced Leslie to the deck side of the dance floor.

"Leslie, this is my man, Jamie Sommers. Jamie, this is Leslie Anderson."

Grenville hoped against hope that he was misreading the phrase on Jamie's T-shirt.

Grenville noticed the hot red flush spreading up from Jamie's neck across his face, and attributed it to his embarrassment at meeting such a lady in such attire.

"Glad to meet you," Jamie said politely. "Grenville, could I speak to you for a minute?"

"Certainly. Excuse me, Leslie, I'll only be a moment."

Leslie found a chair to watch the dance floor, and Jamie and Grenville walked to the railing overlooking the night sea.

"Goddamn it, Grenville!" Jamie spoke though gritted teeth. "I'm not your fucking man! Stop calling me that! I hate it. 'My man'—you might as well call me a fuckin' dog and get it right!"

Grenville stood amazed. Jamie had never spoken to him like that. Once the sheer surprise was over, Grenville said, "Jamie!" in a tone that made the young man's knees turn to jelly, made him grab the railing.

Jamie, suddenly frightened, blinked back tears.

"It ain't fair, Grenville," he said. "You get mad at me all the time. Can't I be mad at you once in a while?"

He looked out across the ocean, afraid to meet Grenville's eyes.

Grenville was thinking he actually preferred this little spat of anger to Jamie's usual muttering sulks.

"First of all, how exactly would you like to be introduced? In my day it was common to refer to one's manservant as 'my man.' But if you prefer something else . . . just exactly what would you like to be called?"

Jamie, a little heartened by the lack of rage in Grenville's voice, thought: Chauffeur? Cook? Repairman? Restorer? Errand boy?

"How about Jamie Sommers? Okay? Just Jamie Sommers."

"All right. And exactly when and where did you inform me that the phrase 'my man' was so offensive to you?"

Jamie's eyes went wide. He had never mentioned that title

grated so strongly—he never had the courage. Suddenly he thought, I could have just told him, a long time ago, instead of getting madder and madder about it.

"So you'll concede that this is the first I've heard of it? I will take note. Now, surely you didn't call me out here to discuss your job description?"

"Oh." Jamie remembered. "No—you know I didn't come in last night?"

"Yes," Grenville said dryly. "I noticed."

"Well, I got another invite for tonight. So I thought I'd tell you. So maybe if you wanted to have somebody in for a brandy or something . . ."

Jamie's voice trailed off. Then he finished, "Anyway, I won't be barging in."

He was as red as he had been before.

Grenville paused. Of all the impertinent . . . but Jamie was just trying to be thoughtful, in his own blundering way.

"Thank you, Jamie. I'll see you sometime tomorrow." Grenville left Jamie standing at the railing, the cool night air taking the heat from his face.

A nightcap, Grenville thought. A pleasant idea.

Jamie and the girls danced all the way to the cabin from the disco, where they'd danced for hours before.

"Oh man, am I tired," Jamie said, sitting on a bunk, his head spinning from beer, scotch, and music.

"Too tired?" Michelle pulled off her T-shirt, unzipped her jeans.

"Naw," Jamie said, hoping he was right.

Diane, still dancing, paused to kiss the top of Jamie's head.

"Listen, you girls have been awful sweet to me. Anything special you like? Just tell ol' Jamie. Anything at all."

Diane stopped dancing. She and Michelle looked at each other.

"Well," Michelle said, "instead of us telling you . . ."

"We could show you," Diane finished.

Jamie suddenly felt very alert, almost sober, not tired at all.

Diane unzipped her minidress and let it fall to the floor. Michelle jumped onto the bunk across from Jamie, and Diane crawled in beside her.

"So show me," Jamie said. "I'll take notes."

They did.

"Good evening, Grenville."

Grenville turned to see Jamie joining him at the sedate first-class bar.

At least he was presentably dressed in slacks and polo shirt, Grenville thought.

He hadn't seen Jamie for days, except to pass him at the pool, see him in the horrible pizza parlor, playing some game called Ping-Pong—each time Jamie was behaving in a disgustingly familiar way with a couple of young women.

Grenville couldn't even tell from his behavior or theirs which was the girlfriend.

But the voyage was turning out much better than he'd hoped—partly because of Leslie, the very personification of the saying "Lady in the parlor . . ."

And partly because Jamie was in his own cabin only long

enough to shower and shave. Unfailingly neat in Hawkes Hall, here Jamie left the small bathroom a pigsty.

Grenville thought he should be able to civilly converse with Jamie for a few minutes—then changed his mind as he realized Jamie was already quite drunk.

"I'll have what he's havin'," Jamie told the bartender.

He took a sip of the small glass set in front of him and violently grimaced.

"What the hell is this?"

"Sherry."

"Geez, you drinkin' or cookin'? Here, take mine. I'll have a Chivas," he told the bartender.

Grenville frowned, a thought trying to form . . .

"So, Grenville. How's it going?"

"Quite well," Grenville said. "These stabilizers are amazing. Very different from passenger ships in the eighteenth century."

"I bet," Jamie said. They remained silent for a moment.

Jamie was thinking that two girls were even more fun than he'd hoped, and no problem at all.

Michelle was so sweet, she'd melt in your arms like sugar in warm rain. Diane was very athletic, with a wicked sense of humor. Except for being scrupulously careful of whose turn it was to finish with him—and fortunately they didn't expect him to keep track—they were happily content to share. And they had the best way of waking him from a bad dream. . . .

"The girls are trying on clothes," Jamie said. "They got off the boat today to shop. I took a nap. There's no room in there for me, they got stuff piled all over. You guys get off the boat?"

"We went sightseeing. Visited a museum." Grenville tried not to be offended by the phrase "you guys."

No doubt this was the kind of conversation Jamie had with his peers.

"Tell me, Grenville." Jamie sipped philosophically at his scotch. "I know you're cured and all that, but do you ever kind of get the urge to bite somebody? Just for old time's sake?"

Grenville blinked, unable to believe what he was hearing. Then he said, "If I ever do, Jamie, once again you'll be first on the list. Just for old time's sake."

Grenville took a malicious satisfaction in the fleeting look of terror on Jamie's face, the long swallow he took from his drink.

The glass shook a little as Jamie set it back on the bar and motioned for another.

Grenville decided he'd said enough to shut Jamie up, and raised his glass.

"So Grenville," Jamie said conversationally, "yours give good head?"

Jamie never thought he'd see Grenville spew a drink all over a bar, and thought it was worth it if he was killed for it. He had to laugh, although he also had to clutch the bar, expecting to feel those iron fingers gripping his throat.

No one else was near, the bartender busy elsewhere, and Grenville took his cocktail napkin to his mouth.

"Jamie," he said, his voice muffled, "go while you can."

Jamie didn't have to be told twice, even though he'd heard, in the deep voice of anger, the unmistakable sound of laughter.

Grenville entered his cabin intending to read his *Wall Street Journal* on the shaded balcony.

Leslie was taking her parents on a glass bottom–boat excursion—entirely too much sun for him to tolerate. Though it was no longer fatal, direct heavy sun was never comfortable. But perhaps that was just his East Coast upbringing. . . .

He paused, hearing a sound from what he took to be a pile of dirty wet laundry on Jamie's unused bunk—on second glance it turned out to be Jamie himself.

Sobbing uncontrollably.

"Jamie?" He took a step nearer. "What's wrong?"

Jamie's voice, distorted by the pillow, by tears, told him nothing; Grenville listened to the distasteful sailor vocabulary without learning any more than Jamie was in extreme distress.

His first thought was to take his *Wall Street Journal* and go—perhaps Jamie had had a quarrel with those brazen young women—surely he'd prefer to be alone . . .

Jamie rolled to a sitting position on the bunk, still hugging the pillow.

"Grenville, I can't fuckin' swim anymore." He sobbed, in that heartbreaking, confiding voice he'd sometimes used since leaving Terrace View.

Like Grenville was his best friend in the whole wide world. Like he could tell him anything.

Louisa said that was one way of Jamie's dealing with their past relationship—if Jamie *voluntarily* made himself dependent on Grenville, twisted their past bond into one of deep friendship, it gave him a measure of control.

There was a whole new name for this behavior, studied more since the war—post-traumatic stress syndrome. Louisa said Jamie was classic.

Whatever it was, the rare times Jamie used that tone Grenville felt unbearably guilty.

Sighing, he sat down on the bunk—as far away as he could, since Jamie, T-shirt, cutoffs and all, was soaking wet.

"What do you mean?" Grenville said.

"I can't—my shoulder, it catches my shoulder, the goddamn fuckin' bullet holes—my whole back froze up and I almost fuckin' drowned—those asshole cops—I was a good swimmer, a motherfuckin' great swimmer. Kellen always said you couldn't sink me with an anchor—I was pearl diving in fuckin' Tahiti and those guys said I was good—now—my whole right shoulder's useless—feels like I'm bein' knifed."

Jamie choked out his pain and despair.

"Let me make sure I understand you. You can't swim anymore? This is the first you've tried since the shooting? Jamie, that's been years."

"Well, where am I gonna swim around Hawkes Harbor? It's got that weird current and it's colder than . . ." He wiped his face on the pillow.

His shoulder bothered him a lot when he had to do lifting, digging, physical labor—the shoulder blade was shattered, muscle and nerve had knit back over sharp edges of bone—sometimes it ached so badly he couldn't sleep. It was one of the main reasons for his addiction to muscle relaxants.

But he never dreamed it could stop him midstroke after diving into thirty feet of ocean, he forgot about his damaged lung . . . His whole back cramped, he'd barely made it to the surface.

If Michelle hadn't had lifeguard training . . .

"You know what that's like? To be really, really good at somethin' and then find out you can't do it anymore?" Jamie raised his tearstained face. "It was something I was great at and now I can't fuckin' swim."

"Actually, Jamie," Grenville said. "I am relieved. For a moment I thought you were referring to fucking."

Jamie's reaction to hearing Grenville say that word for the first time was the same as if he'd been slapped.

Wordless, knocked out of hysteria, he stared at Grenville. After a minute, he half laughed.

"That sounds like something Kell would say."

Grenville disliked intensely being compared to that blackmailing scum Kellen Quinn, who'd more than justified every eighteenth-century prejudice against the Irish that Grenville had ever harbored—but Jamie evidently meant it as a compliment, so Grenville tried to take it that way. "Jamie, I know it must be a shock to you, but you do realize you have little need for swimming these days. . . ."

Jamie slowly shook his head.

"You don't get it, Grenville. It was one of . . . I don't have a lot of stuff to be proud of like you do . . ."

He stood up.

"I'm gonna take a shower."

Grenville left the damp bunk to sit in one of the lounge chairs on the balcony. He stared at the *Wall Street Journal* without reading.

He felt rather ill.

There was a frantic pounding on the door of the cabin. Grenville opened it to face those two friends of Jamie's.

They were still in their beach clothes, one of them openly crying, the other close to it.

"Is Jamie here? Is he okay?"

"Yes. He's showering at the mo—"

They pushed by him without ceremony, threw open the bathroom door.

Grenville stood aghast.

Jamie, drying himself off, dropped the towel, startled to have the girls fling themselves on him.

"Don't be upset, Jamie."

"It's okay, we don't care."

"It's not your fault."

They hugged him fiercely, kissed him frantically, and he put an arm around each of them, pulling them close.

"Please don't be sad."

"It doesn't matter."

"We want you to be happy."

"Okay," Jamie said. He kissed each of them. "I'm okay. Don't worry."

He was still red-eyed but was no longer sobbing.

"Hey, I'm okay. Come on, we'll go to the Sugar Shack again tonight. Okay? Shut 'em down."

They seemed reluctant to release him, but he gradually pulled one from his neck, the other off his waist.

"Come to our cabin right away?"

"Please, it's empty without you."

"Sure," Jamie said.

"Right away. Don't forget."

"I'll be there in five minutes. Promise."

He gently herded them out of the bathroom and shut the door.

The girls looked at Grenville apologetically.

"Sorry, Mr. Hawkes."

"We didn't mean to disturb you."

"We just . . ."

"Wanted to see Jamie."

"He's the nicest person . . ."

"The sweetest guy . . ."

"But you know that . . ."

"We just love him."

They left, leaving the room smelling of suntan lotion and seawater.

In a moment Jamie came out, a towel wrapped around his waist, and went to paw through his laundry stack, looking for something relatively clean.

He dug out a pair of jeans, a purple T-shirt.

Grenville smothered a gasp at the sight of Jamie's mutilated back.

Oh, good God, he had never dreamed it had been that bad . . . though at the time no one thought he would live through it, not a doctor thought he could survive . . .

Yet Grenville had suspected he would, having realized very early that Jamie Sommers was a survivor.

"Jamie."

Jamie looked at him, apprehensive. He knew Grenville couldn't stand scenes, he'd probably had all he could tolerate for one day.

"You are mistaken. You have much to be proud of."

Jamie blinked hard. "Thanks."

Jamie rolled the T-shirt down over his head, pulled on his jeans without bothering with underwear. He stuck his feet into flip-flops.

"See you around, Grenville," he said.

"Yes, Jamie. See you around."

Sussex Airport, Delaware
AUGUST 1968

Louisa Kahne was a little late. Jamie and Grenville had already left the plane as she reached the gate.

"I'll take it out of your wages for the next five years—no, ten—my God, Jamie you must have been drinking like the proverbial fish to run up a bill like that! Did you never draw a sober breath the whole time?"

"I don't think that's fair. You never told me drinks were separate. I thought they were included. You said it was my vacation, too. . . . Hey, Louisa."

Grenville stopped to give Louisa a quick hug and a kiss on the cheek. She squeezed him back and turned to Jamie.

"Jamie Sommers, you must have put on ten pounds."

Jamie felt self-consciously at the small roll around his waist.

"Well, Louisa, there wasn't a whole lot to do on that ship besides eat and fu—lay around." He caught himself.

She didn't miss the unsaid word or the quick glance he and Grenville exchanged, but ignored both.

"Well, you do look relaxed." And she noted, not the least bit nervous.

"If he were any more relaxed, he'd be dead," Grenville commented dryly.

Grenville looked well, too. Not tan and pudgy like Jamie, but much less grim and tense. And something else . . . she realized he was wearing a blazer over an open-necked polo shirt—it was the first time she'd seen him travel in anything other than a business suit.

It was only too becoming . . . but she frowned, suspecting the hand of a woman.

Louisa suddenly wondered suspiciously what exactly had gone on during the cruise.

Both men had an unmistakable, gleefully guilty look.

And as she joined them at the baggage claim from a trip to the ladies' room, she heard Grenville say, in a voice of awe:

"Both? Actually?"

And Jamie chuckle wickedly. "Oh, yeah."

This was the last time, she thought, that she'd send those two off together.

Entirely too much male bonding.

The three stood silently waiting for the luggage to appear.

Grenville was thinking how good it was to see Louisa again. Leslie had been very dear, but there were so many things she didn't know about him, could never know.

Louisa knew the worst and loved him in spite of it. He could share anything with her. He realized how lucky he was to have her in his life.

In one of his rare gestures of affection, he put his arm around her. She leaned against his side.

Jamie watched them absently. Those two together always seemed so *right* to him. . . .

Jamie was thinking he needed a girlfriend. Sex was great, but what he was going to miss most was waking up to soft girl bodies snuggled on him, going to sleep in their arms. That was what he'd miss the most. That and the sex.

He had mooned around about Katie Roddendem long enough. Maybe he never would be over her completely, but he could be happy again.

But then, there was no rush.

The girls had promised to visit. He'd better rest up.

"It's nice to be back," he said, at the same moment as Grenville.

Like they were somehow connected. Like there was some kind of bond.

Hawkes Harbor

"I toldja, Louisa, you want me to work for you, you have to make an appointment, pay me. And I'm getting booked up."

"Jamie, this is an important project with a tight deadline—it is incredibly cold down here."

Louisa shivered, wrapping her coat tightly around her.

"That's why I'm fixing the furnace," Jamie said patiently. "It's an important project with a tight deadline, too. School's back in session Monday and it's twenty degrees out."

"I didn't think the school had a budget that could accommodate paying *you* by the hour," she said tartly.

"I charge by the job," he said. "I know I'm slow."

Louisa bit her lip. She didn't mean to hurt him. Jamie could be so exasperating, but she was very fond of him, too.

"Grenville doesn't mind you taking outside jobs?" she asked, curious.

She and Grenville had both been surprised when Jamie had fliers printed advertising his services for hire, had rented a post-office box for messages. Grenville refused to question him about it, but Louisa was dying to know. . . .

"Not as long as I've got everything taken care of at the Hall. I'm just working extra on my time off."

If he minds he can give me a goddamn raise, Jamie thought. He'd needed some extra money, figured out a way to make it; it wasn't their business.

Except for his motives.

"Jamie," she said—something in his quiet defiance, his strangely confident air, aroused her suspicions. "Just why exactly is it that you need more money?"

"Everybody can always use more money."

"Well, it's not like you pay room and board."

She sounded just like Grenville, he thought. Like the freezing dimly lit isolated Hawkes Hall was the fucking Ritz.

"Mr. Sommers!" Another voice spoke loudly from behind him. Jamie jumped, dropped his wrench on his foot, and hopped around, trying to keep from swearing and not doing a very good job.

He hadn't heard anyone come down the stairs. Louisa might have warned him. . . .

"You are just the man I wanted to see."

Jamie turned, rubbing at his foot through his boot.

It was one of the schoolteachers, a short, dark, mushroom-shaped woman he'd seen that morning upstairs. She was busy going through desks, cleaning out trash—since Wilson, the regular janitor, was in the hospital, the teachers were having to do things like that.

Jamie had made it clear to the principal; he was a repairman, not a janitor. He hoped she wasn't expecting him to mop her room.

"Hello," Louisa said, extending her hand. "I'm Louisa Kahne."

"Oh yes yes yes, everyone knows who you are. I'm Lucinda Maples, I teach fourth- and fifth-grade English, and I am also in charge of all the plays, the drama department. And when I saw you this morning, Mr. Sommers, I thought, there is the man I wanted to see."

She fixed him with her bright dark eyes.

Jamie wrung his hands together, wiped the palms on his pants. Busy women like this made him nervous, gave him flashbacks to the nuns. He suddenly felt trapped down there with her and Louisa—I'd rather be locked up with a vampire, he thought.

"I want you to help us with the scenery. And the props."

"The scenery?"

"She means for the plays, Jamie," Louisa explained.

Jamie was irritated. She was always treating him like a moron. He would have figured it out.

"Yes, our props right now are pitiful, the children would love something more elaborate, like the sets they see on TV. I've toured the Hall, I know what you can do—you are quite marvelous at woodcraft."

"Well, thanks, but . . ."

"Of course it would be pro bono—there's barely any budget for materials."

"That means—"

"I know what it means, Louisa."

"But you would be giving to the community, practicing good citizenship, and the children would be so pleased. And, it wouldn't be so very time-consuming."

"It ain't—isn't the time, Miss Maples."

"I think there's a way you could use it as a tax write-off. Mr. Hawkes might know."

Yeah, if it's a write-off I bet he does, Jamie thought. "No, it's not the money either."

"Well what? Speak up!"

Jamie felt like he was back in a classroom, about to get whacked with a ruler.

"I-I-I d-d-don't think the parents would like it. Me bein' around their kids."

"What on earth are you talking about?"

Louisa was looking at him strangely, too.

"I mean, everybody knows I was a mental patient. . . ."

"So? There are several people in this town who have been mental patients. Sometimes I think there is something in the water. . . . And, there are several more who *should* be. No one thinks anything of *that*."

"Well, and lot of people thought I was the person who kidnapped Katie Roddendem. . . ."

"Mr. Sommers, you are deluded if you think people believe that. Katie Roddendem Morgan will tell anyone who listens that you are one of her dearest friends."

For a second, the sudden surge of love and gratitude he felt toward Katie overwhelmed his senses; he felt tears jump to his eyes.

"And the Hawkeses have trusted you with their little prince and heir for years."

Jamie realized she meant Ricky.

"Quite frankly, the town has had other things to talk about for some time now, Mr. Sommers."

Jamie remembered to shut his mouth. Grenville told him often enough it made him look like an imbecile to stand around slack-jawed. If what she said was true . . .

Then when Mr. Garvey said, "How's it going, Jamie? What you planting this year?" he was inquiring, not feeling sorry for the poor loser Jamie.

And when Mayor Wells sat next to him at the counter in the Coffee Shoppe, and said, "What ya think, Jamie, we ever going to get any rain?" he was asking for an opinion, not checking up on lowlife Sommers.

And Riley, at the gas station, who kept bugging him to join the bowling team—

The people who said, "Good morning, Jamie. What's Mr. Hawkes up to these days?" weren't secretly afraid of him, or despising him, or even thinking about him much.

He was just another citizen of Hawkes Harbor. He was awed by the thought.

"Well, uh, okay." He managed not to stammer.

"Good. Meet me upstairs in the gymnasium when you're finished here. We can start with the Christmas pageant. I have a wonderful idea for the manger. . . ."

When she left, Jamie picked up his wrench and wondered what it was he'd been doing before she assailed him. The pipes?

"Well, that should be a treat for you. Much more fun than helping me."

He jumped and managed to dodge the wrench. He'd forgotten all about Louisa.

"Well, it might be."

At least making scenery sounded like more fun than unpacking volumes, artifacts, filing documents. Otherwise, he couldn't see much difference really, in being bossed by one woman or the other.

"You never did tell me why you've needed extra money."

"Well, I don't have to. But I guess it is your business in a way. I got a lot of lawyer bills to pay."

Louisa was as astounded as he'd hoped.

"Legal bills? Why on earth would you need a lawyer?"

Jamie thought about saying, "To sue you, like Dr. McDevitt suggested."

But he didn't. Louisa could be exasperating, but he was very fond of her, too. He didn't want to hurt her feelings.

And he knew what he'd done would anger her.

"Last week me and Leonard Pagano went up to Terrace View to see Dr. McDevitt. He gave me every test he could think of, and he said I was probably the sanest person in Hawkes Harbor. Having a bad memory, being a little bit nervous don't make you crazy, he said.

"I ain't in your custody anymore, Louisa, and I got papers and legal witness. You want a forcible commitment, you'll have to go through the courts, and prove me a danger to myself or others, and Dr. McDevitt will show up at any hearing. And he's on my side. And my lawyer will be there, too.

"So don't tell me you're gonna send me back to Terrace View

anymore, Louisa. You're not sending me anywhere. Not ever."

Louisa's jaw dropped. First at his audacity, then at the realization he'd taken her seriously all these years.

Grenville is right, Jamie thought absently. You do look stupid standing around with your mouth hanging open.

He wasn't going to tell her all of what Dr. McDevitt had told him—Louisa's days of running Terrace View were over.

"She's not a bad person, Doc."

"No, Jamie, and she is a very good anthropologist. But she has no business dealing with patients and you very well know it. And now her grandfather knows it, too."

Still, Jamie thought, let him tell her. This will be bad enough.

He braced himself, knowing nothing angered Louisa Kahne more than any loss of power; he watched her search her mind for the next plan of attack, knowing what she would come up with—

"What's Grenville going to think of all this? He's going to be furious."

Jamie swallowed, though he had prepared for that possibility.

"Well, Louisa, Grenville may be mad at me, maybe he'll even fire me.

"I just don't think he's going to kill me anymore."

Louisa Kahne was speechless.

Later that night at dinner, she recounted to Grenville the whole episode—with much heat, and a little exaggeration of Jamie's disrespectful attitude.

He listened in silence, nodding.

Finally she sputtered to a stop.

"Well?" she said.

"You don't suppose we'll have to attend school plays just to view his handiwork, do you?"

"No, I mean, what do you think about the other—"

"I think I'll give him a raise," Grenville said. "He shouldn't have to take extra jobs on his days off."

He paused. "I wish he'd asked my advice about a lawyer. Pagano's fees are outrageous."

The money was welcome, but Jamie appreciated the gesture much more.

Day After Christmas

The Boardinghouse
Hawkes Harbor, Delaware
CHRISTMAS DAY, 1978

"It always beats me why you two would rather eat Christmas dinner here than up at the Manor."

Mrs. Pivens handed Jamie the sweet potatoes.

"Food's better," Jamie said. He looked up at the late arrival,
annoyed.

"I had to put in an appearance, sorry. The company's better,
too." Rick Hawkes flung himself into a kitchen chair, yanking at

his tie. He winked at Trisha. She tried to ignore him but couldn't help a smirk.

"I'd be in the kitchen with the rest of the staff," Jamie said. "They're snobbier than the Hawkeses themselves. Noses so up in the air they'd drown in a rain. And here nobody's going to count the silverware after I leave."

"And nobody's going to gasp and cry if I break a priceless antique whatever that we only use for Christmas." Rick went on with the list of why the boardinghouse Christmas dinner was better than the elegant affair at the Manor.

"In an hour Father will be drunk and quarreling with Aunt Lydia. Barbara has brought home some freak she's found at Berkeley. The Boston branch is sitting there horrified. At least I think that's it. They're so inbred that may be the only expression they can come up with. Louisa and Grenville are already snipping at each other—are they ever going to get married, Jamie?"

"I doubt it," Jamie said. "Grenville's pretty set in his ways. 'Sides, he's been married twice before. He does like to rile her up, though."

"Can't blame *her* for trying," Trisha said. "He's still the sexiest man in town."

Mrs. Pivens laughed, while Rick made a growl of protest.

"Oh sorry," Trisha corrected. *"Jamie."*

"Really, Jamie, how old is Grenville, anyway?"

"A little older than he looks," Jamie said blandly. "A little long in the tooth."

He fought a snort of laughter as Trisha's mouth fell open, as Rick stuttered for a change of subject. He'd always wondered how much those two knew . . . when Rick was just a kid . . .

"Father says I can't go to Fort Lauderdale for spring break."

Rick found a new subject. "He wants me to go to London. For business! London! It won't even be spring there! Is there any ham left?"

"Anyway," he resumed, sliding back in the chair with a plateful of ham and turkey and mashed potatoes, "Grenville was on my side. Said London would be cold and rainy."

"He's right," Jamie said. London had never been one of his favorite places. "You need to go somewhere warm. Too bad Havana—"

Jamie stopped abruptly. He had a vivid memory—not of Havana, where he'd never been, but of a hot dusty train car in the south of France. He could hear Kell's voice so clearly, over the rattle of the train. Kellen—describing Havana—the beaches, the palm trees, the soft hot nights, the nightclubs. He could almost smell the flowers, the women, the fancy cigars. . . . "It's too bad you missed Cuba in its heyday, Jamie. The women in Havana are just your type."

They'd gone to New Orleans, instead, he and Kell. Jamie hadn't been too much older than Rick, then.

Strange he'd think of Kellen Quinn all of a sudden. He hadn't thought of him in a while.

"New Orleans is a fun city."

"Good idea. I've always wanted to go there."

Jamie remembered, as from another life, his cocaine- and rum-fueled blast through New Orleans. He'd been blowing his share of the loot from that gun-smuggling deal . . . couldn't get rid of that money fast enough . . .

"You're better off in Fort Lauderdale, though, kid." Jamie suddenly didn't want Rick in New Orleans. Florida would be wild enough.

Geez, I'm turning into an old fart, Jamie thought. And I'm not even forty, yet.

Rick said, "That will be about time to fit up the boat."

"You won't be home till summer, and not much then," Trisha pointed out.

"I don't care—when I am home, I'll want the boat. And I expect Jamie and you to keep it seaworthy."

"I won't be home much either," Trisha said. "You're not the only college student in this town. Looks like Jamie's stuck with it."

"Guess so."

Rick still insisted no one else take care of his boat. This care included Jamie taking the boat for a sail on his days off. Rick, in reality, didn't have much time to sail anymore but made sure Jamie had a legitimate excuse to use the boat.

The Hawkeses had a kind streak but seemed terrified that someone would find out.

"Were you at the shelter this morning?" Rick handed the apple pie around.

"Just for a couple of hours. Christmas, Thanksgiving, we get a lot of volunteers," Jamie answered. "Wish they'd remember people are homeless other days of the year."

"You know, you never have been able to get Grenville down there." Trisha slyly caught Rick's eye. Jamie's inability to tolerate the least criticism of Grenville had been a family joke for years.

Once Rick tried to laugh about it to Grenville. Grenville had gazed at him with eyes of winter midnight and said, "Jamie's loyalty has always been one of his most estimable qualities. One we would all do well to emulate." Rick was uncomfortable enough with the look, the tone, the words, to never bring it up again.

As if cued, Jamie said, "Grenville writes us some nice-size checks. That's hard enough for him. People help in different ways."

He took a bite of pie. "It's not like I see your young smart asses down there helping, either."

They ate in silence for a moment. Then Mrs. Pivens cleared her throat.

"We enjoyed the Christmas pageant this year."

"Nobody fell off the stage and broke their arm. That's all I ever ask."

Jamie still couldn't figure out how the job of making scenery had turned into the job of assistant stage manager for the school plays. The job mainly consisted of helping Miss Maples herd kids on and off the stage, hissing lines to terrified performers.

"Mickey was a darling angel," Mrs. Pivens said.

Jamie laughed. "He's a little hell-raiser."

"Must get it from Katie," Trisha said.

"Wait till two years from now, when you get the twins," Mrs. Pivens said. "Katie and Mitch are bringing them all by a little later."

"I guess you know, Katie's started on her fourth," Jamie said. "Says she can already tell it's another boy."

Mrs. Pivens gave him a sympathetic look, but before anyone could say anything, Jamie got up, searched the fridge, and held up an icy bottle of champagne.

"Some Christmas cheer."

"This looks like good stuff." Rick eyed the foil label.

"One of my chores this week was picking up the Christmas liquor," Jamie said. "I thought a tip was in order."

Grenville had agreed.

The cork made a satisfying explosion.

"Merry Christmas."

———

When Jamie pulled the car around to the front entrance of the Manor, Grenville and Louisa were already down the steps. Lydia and Richard waved from the doorway, then the ponderous door swung shut.

Jamie opened the back door of the black Mercedes sedan.

"Do you think you are capable of driving us home?"

"More capable than you are," Jamie said. Grenville could drink anyone in town under the table, but his driving skills left much to be desired.

"Hop in."

"Honestly, Jamie, have you ever seen Grenville hop?" Louisa asked in all seriousness.

Jamie thought it better not to answer.

He stopped at the Lodge.

"Jamie," Louisa said, "if you ever get that firewood, you are under no circumstances to help unload it."

"I concur." Grenville opened the door for Louisa. "You are no longer five and twenty, and with your bad back . . ."

Jamie remained silent as they went into the Lodge. If Grenville did not return in ten minutes, Jamie knew to drive home alone. They should have gotten married a long time ago, Jamie thought. Then we'd have a little Hawkes running around the Hall I could teach to sail. . . .

After a short time, Grenville joined Jamie in the front seat.

Jamie had made the drive between the Manor, the Lodge, and Hawkes Hall so many times he could have done it far drunker than he was now. He parked in front of the Hall and went around to open the door for Grenville—it was habit, Grenville no longer required servantlike behavior from him.

"Jamie." Grenville frowned at him.

Once that frown could make him cringe, but now Jamie realized Grenville just had too much port and was trying to think.

No longer monster. No longer God.

"What?" Jamie gave him a hand out of the car.

"Look in the trunk."

"The trunk?"

"I ordered you a Christmas present and forgot to give it to you this morning."

"Yeah?" Jamie was astonished. He hadn't expected anything; Grenville wasn't in the habit of giving him presents, unless it was clothes—Grenville didn't think Jamie's wardrobe suitable to his station a lot of times—but Jamie couldn't remember a Christmas present other than a bonus.

"B-b-but I didn't get you anything." He hated it when his old stammer reappeared.

"Don't be absurd. Open the trunk."

Absurd; hell, Jamie thought. He'd go out and get Grenville a present tomorrow. He'd show him—

He looked uncomprehendingly at the bundle in the trunk. Grenville lifted it out.

"It's a goose-down quilt."

"Yeah?"

Geez, Jamie thought. We're both drunk. He took the bulky blanket. It was surprisingly lightweight.

"Last month, when that insufferable woman from the historical society was going through the house, I noticed what a draft comes through your chimney. Your fire goes out before morning, doesn't it?"

"Yeah," Jamie said. He was dumbfounded. He always did wake up cold, no matter how carefully he made up his fire. He couldn't remember a warm night at Hawkes Hall. Even in summer it held a chill. Too many trees. Too many secrets.

"Well, this should help."

"Yeah." Jamie hugged the quilt.

"Shall we go in before we freeze?" Grenville said.

Like he ever felt the cold, Jamie thought. The sharp wind made his eyes water, and he wiped them on the quilt.

Hawkes Hall, Hawkes Harbor, Delaware
December 26, 1978

Jamie woke and dozed. A good morning. No bad dreams. Not the good one, either, but maybe tonight . . . No dread of the day. Not too much of a hangover. No freezing chills.

Damn quilt works like insulation, he thought, and as always, thanked God he knew who he was, where he was, why he was.

He never took that for granted. Always grateful for the gift of memory, flawed as it was.

And this morning, he was grateful for a lot of things, this quilt being at the top of the list. He rolled over to look at his clock and as usual, got distracted by pictures. His nightstand was crowded with photos these days, not pill bottles.

The group shot of the Christmas-pageant cast—the entire elementary school, Miss Maples on the top row, Jamie at the bottom. He changed that one every year, putting the old one in an album.

The one Rick took, of Jamie and Michelle and Diane clowning around on the sailboat. That one always made him smile.

Dr. McDevitt and his wife, taken on his around-the-world retirement cruise.

Katie—at her wedding. It had been the first formal occasion Jamie had ever attended, and he was as nervous as Mitch, and surprisingly, *for* Mitch.

In the reception line, he'd shook the lawman's hand, muttered, "Congratulations." Gave Katie a chaste peck on the cheek but couldn't speak—

She'd cried, "Oh Jamie!" and thrown her arms around his neck in a fierce embrace—

The photographer caught the moment.

The look on Mitch's face was priceless.

And Katie was so radiant—

One of his favorites was the black-and-white shot of Grenville that Michelle took, her first visit.

Copies hung in the library at the Manor, in Louisa's office at the Lodge. Michelle wanted it in her published collection, but Jamie'd asked her to leave it out.

Grenville in the great hall of Hawkes Hall, in his black silk smoking jacket, reading by candle- and firelight. It caught the essence of the man, was a stunning piece of art, but what caused the greatest controversy was behind him, in the shadows of the corner, you could see if you looked carefully, the transparent figure of Sophia Marie.

Richard Hawkes always declared he saw nothing—yet refused to hang one in the office gallery.

Everyone else was awed by it. . . .

Jamie was so warm it would be hard to get up . . . then he saw his clock. "Holy shit!" Ten o'clock! He was normally up at seven A.M.

"I'm sorry," he stammered, rushing past Grenville, who sat sipping coffee in the kitchen. "I musta forgot to turn on the alarm."

"Don't worry, Jamie," Grenville said, without a trace of malice. "You'll be sorrier when you taste what I've concocted for coffee."

Jamie found no sign of breakfast in the kitchen, except for a pot of coffee. He poured himself a cup and sat down. Grenville turned the page of the newspaper.

"If that quilt is going to become a problem with your rising on time, I might take it back," Grenville said.

Jamie took a sip of coffee and nearly choked. Grenville couldn't boil water, he thought.

"You're not getting it back. First time I've ever been warm in the morning. You want me to fix breakfast?"

"Well, maybe the day after Christmas is still a sort of holiday," Grenville said. "I just rose a short while ago myself. Let's go have breakfast in Hawkes Harbor."

They ordered ham and eggs and waffles and more coffee at the Coffee Shoppe. Jamie was mildly hungover, but not too hungover to notice some stares they were getting.

Everyone connected them—Jamie was fully aware that anytime his name was mentioned—Jamie Sommers—"who works for Grenville Hawkes" was added onto it.

He didn't mind. There were worse things they could have added, he thought, had things gone the way they were going before he met Grenville. . . .

They were rarely seen in public together though, and Jamie was getting a kick out of the hushed whispers going around the café. Grenville was a Hawkes, a well-known business tycoon, with ties to the government, a big man around Hawkes Harbor. It was like being with a celebrity.

And no matter how well it was known that Jamie worked for Grenville, it would occur to few that Grenville actually *talked* to him.

"So, you got anything for me to do today? I was going to wrap the pipes. There's a cold front comin' in." Jamie had awakened thinking about insulation. He didn't want to deal with busted pipes, especially since being in the basement still gave him the creeps.

"Would you drive me into D.C.? I have an afternoon appointment and frankly don't feel up to the drive."

"Too much Christmas cheer?" Jamie grinned, liking the way he'd been asked instead of ordered, although of course, it was an order. A pleasant one, too. A long drive in the black Mercedes was hardly a chore. Jamie loved driving the Mercedes. He kept it immaculate. His own car was full of odds and ends of lumber, tools, fast-food wrappers.

The D.C. traffic made him a little nervous, but he'd deal with that when he got there.

Grenville scowled slightly.

"I believe I am much more seasoned than you are."

"Yeah, and not many people are," Jamie said. "Sure, I'll drive ya."

Tomorrow would be a better day to wrap pipe, anyway. The cleaning crew was coming, Jamie'd have to be at home to supervise. The basement wasn't so bad if there were people in the house. And surely Davis would show up with that overdue firewood. . . .

It was a comfortable drive, though silent. Grenville looked over stock reports, shuffled through spreadsheets, rarely glancing at the snow piled high off the sides of the highway. The snow was days old, deep and heavy, but the plows had cleared the roads long ago.

Jamie had driven this route many times; he let his mind wander. He kept thinking about the goose-down quilt, it was funny that Grenville would realize he needed it.

He was still determined to get Grenville a Christmas present. A book would be good. God knew Grenville couldn't seem to get enough of them. He should have thought to ask Louisa . . . hell, he could pick one out himself.

"Drop me off at the office building on the corner."

Jamie wove through the downtown traffic. It was a little heavier than the usual Tuesday traffic—people shopping sales, returning Christmas gifts. Grenville took a tablet from the glove compartment and began writing.

"Could you meet me on the twenty-second floor around five o'clock? I should be through by then. We can go somewhere decent for dinner."

They had agreed to skip lunch, since breakfast was so late.

"Okay," Jamie said. Grenville handed him the sheet of paper before he got out—it contained the time and place of their meeting.

Jamie's short-term memory was vastly improved, but they had both learned to use this backup.

Jamie found a space in a parking garage and wrote down its address before leaving.

The Christmas decorations were still up in the stores, Christmas carols still blaring. Jamie strolled the streets, looking for a bookstore.

He paused in front of the two-story storefront, sighing at the lines of people waiting to return or exchange their presents. But this would be his only chance.

The history section was easy to find, but Jamie looked hopelessly at all the titles. Then he saw one he knew. He pulled it off the shelf.

A DAY IN LIFE: HAWKES HARBOR 1770
BY LOUISA KAHNE, PH.D.

There was a photo of Louisa on the back flap, her large silver-gray eyes set off by her salt-and-pepper curls. Funny, Jamie rarely noticed what a good-looking woman she was in real life. Jamie turned to the dedication page.

"To my dear friend G. H. with affection and gratitude."

Yeah, she should have affection and gratitude for Grenville, Jamie thought. He'd practically written the book for her.

"We have a few copies of that book autographed by the author. She's a professor at Harvard."

"Yeah." Jamie glanced at the sales clerk. "I know, I gotta autographed copy." *Jamie, who changed history—love, Louisa.* That was what she'd written.

Jamie didn't enjoy reading, and even if he had, after all these years with Grenville, 1770 bored the hell out of him. But his copy of *A Day in Life* was one of his most treasured possessions.

"What would you recommend for somebody who liked this book?" he asked.

The clerk pulled out three others, and Jamie looked through them. He liked books with a lot of pictures. One had pictures of boats, the old sailing rigs, frigates, whalers, battleships, passenger schooners. Jamie sighed. He would love to sail a schooner. . . .

"I'll take this one," he said. He looked at the lines and sighed again. "You guys do gift wrap?"

While he was waiting in line, he pulled out his ballpoint pen and wrote on the inside of the cover:

Merry Christmas Grenville
Thanks for the quilt.
Jamie.

Drawing Room, The Manor
Hawkes Harbor, Delaware
JANUARY 2, 1979

Lydia Hawkes looked up from addressing the thank-you notes.

"Who was that at the door, Richard?"

"Some sort of delivery man, wanting to know where Grenville lived."

Richard poured himself a brandy.

"You know, Lydia, it gave me absolute nightmares, thinking he'd ask for a plot in the family cemetery."

He savored the brandy, as he always did the first taste of the day, as he usually did the twelfth.

"Though how very odd of Grenville, to choose that old graveyard on the island."

Washington, D.C.
DECEMBER 26, 1978

"I'm sure Mr. Hawkes will be out soon," the young secretary told him. The twenty-second floor was a big office. Glass and carpet and wood and plants.

"Please take a seat."

"Okay," Jamie said. He hung his overcoat on the coat rack next to Grenville's. He sank into a sofa and picked up a *Forbes* magazine but couldn't keep from watching the window, where a cold gray day was going into a darker twilight.

"Looks like we might get some more snow." The secretary noticed his nervous glances.

"Yeah," Jamie said.

Sundown was still the worst part of the day for him. The coming of night always made him uneasy. If he were home, back at Hawkes Hall, he'd have something planned to do about now—a tricky piece of carpentry, a huge jigsaw puzzle, a complicated recipe; lately he'd been putting together a ham radio.

Sometimes Grenville would ask him for a game of chess, and by a strange coincidence, it was always that time of the evening. (Viewing the game as a moving puzzle, Jamie had become surprisingly good—he had never beaten Grenville but often gave him a challenging game.)

Anything that would require his full concentration, keeping his mind off the twilight.

But here, there was nothing much to do besides watch it get darker. He noticed the magazine shaking in his hands. He put it down and got up to pace quietly in front of the window. A couple of hours into the night, he'd be okay again. Once he was through the twilight, he could make it through the night.

He never reached for the tranquilizers anymore. And when his shoulder ached, like it was sure to do tonight, after a long day of driving, he took a couple of aspirins.

Jamie thought it ironic, that after spending most of his life with easy access to drugs, that it took doctors and hospitals to turn him into an addict. . . .

Getting off the pills was hard, at first—hell actually—but Jamie was amazed at how much clearer he could think, once his mind was released from the fog. Sometimes he almost felt whole again, sort of like he'd been before the shooting.

He'd never be the same completely. He still had the occasional nightmare that made him (and sometimes Grenville) wake from his screams; he would always startle easy. He cried much easier than he should have—kindness, and paradoxically, deliberate unkindness especially could cause unexpected tears. He had to be careful of what movies he went to, what headlines he glanced at.

He had flashbacks as vivid as time travel.

And even though he knew he could probably burn down the house before Grenville would fire him, he worried too much about losing his job.

Before the shooting . . . he'd been smarter then, but he was wiser now. He wasn't unhappy with the trade.

Jamie started when the office door opened. Grenville came out with another man.

"You drive a hard bargain, Mr. Hawkes," the man was saying.

"I'm sure this way is best for all concerned," Grenville said. It was probably best for Grenville. He liked making money. He liked having money.

Jamie still wished he liked spending it a little better.

"May I present my friend, James Sommers?" Grenville said. "Mr. Graystone."

They shook hands.

"Jamie is actually quite knowledgeable about shipping, himself."

"Really?" Mr. Graystone said. "We must exchange stories sometime."

Jamie nodded, thinking Mr. Graystone would drop dead at some of Jamie's stories.

Yeah, I'm knowledgeable about shipping all right, he thought.

He watched as Grenville made an appointment with the

secretary. She gazed at him with rapt fascination. "I don't care how old he is I'll go out with him if he ever asks," was written all over her face.

She didn't notice Grenville's eyes crinkle with amusement as he said good-bye.

Damn old dog, Jamie thought. What is it with him and women! In the elevator lobby, instead of pushing the button, Grenville walked to the glass wall overlooking the city. Jamie stood beside him.

Almost night now . . .

"It anything like you guys thought it would be?" Jamie asked. "I mean, the government, elections, all that?"

Grenville gave a short laugh. "Not at all. We envisioned nothing this vast, this invasive, this bloated . . . and surely not this corrupt."

"It's better than most countries."

"Yes, yes. I mustn't be run away with youthful idealism at this age. I can still see our dreams under the patina, a pentimento of the vision. And I'll grant you, it's held up amazingly well."

"So, at least there's been progress."

"I'm afraid, Jamie, here as elsewhere, I see inventions, not progress."

As they stood there, gazing out at the lights of the city, Jamie suddenly had a flashback so strong and vivid that he almost dropped to his knees.

A black night, a shivering young man half dead with terror, shock, and loss of blood, and a Monster filled with the rage of two hundred years of confinement; both standing on a windy hillside overlooking the lights of Hawkes Harbor.

It was so real Jamie could smell the sea air, the faint stench of the cemetery, feel the cold dew soaking through his socks, hear his own heart pounding.

And once again a strong grip kept him from falling. Gradually the tightening in his chest relaxed a little.

"Are you quite all right?"

Jamie nodded. He caught his breath.

Did Grenville remember that night? Absently, Jamie rubbed at his throat. The pain had long disappeared, but the scar was still there if you knew where to look.

Abruptly, for no apparent reason, Grenville said, "Do you miss your old life, Jamie?"

Jamie paused. He got nostalgic for it, sometimes. Always a new place to go, always looking for a big score, a little con, sometimes just the next meal. It had been exciting, even exhilarating at times . . . but often not. And so damn aimless . . .

If I had stayed in my old life, Jamie thought, I'd be dead or in prison most likely. The other side of the counter at a shelter.

And even the part he missed most—being on a ship, headed for a strange port—maybe even that would be too much for him now.

It was always the voyage he had loved, never the destination.

Just as Grenville and the Vampire were always two different entities in Jamie's mind, the tough kid Jamie looked back on now no longer seemed like part of himself. . . .

No, the callous young sea tramp, the vengeful monster, were lost somewhere, years ago.

He glanced at Grenville again. *He* was getting older, too, with aches and pains and fears, ebbing strength and faulty memory. Funny, to be cured into old age, pain, and death. But that's the way it was, if you wanted to live life.

"No more than you miss your old life," he answered finally.

"There is much to be said for peace, Jamie."

Jamie had almost forgotten his youthful pondering on the why of it all—was it to help each other find peace?

Grenville put his hand on Jamie's shoulder for a moment, and Jamie blinked back tears. He knew that Grenville remembered everything.

"No, Jamie, not a tree. Not one tree of Hawkes Hall will come down. I like an atmosphere of gentle melancholy," Grenville said.

Jamie sighed. He'd known his landscaping plan wouldn't go over well. "Just to open it up a little around the front? So it won't be so dark and gloomy?"

"If you must dig in the dirt, widen the drive. And I asked you last year to enlarge the garden. But not a tree comes down." He emphasized each word in the last sentence.

"Can't enlarge the garden, there's too much shade." Jamie muttered into his Bloody Mary. Just one, it was a long drive back.

"You should have ordered the scaloppini. It's great."

"You know I detest garlic."

"Thought you were over that."

"*That* has nothing to do with it. I simply dislike garlic. Many people do."

Great, Jamie thought. He was planning on taking Chinese cooking classes in the spring. He remembered how good the food was, in the South China Sea, if you could keep your mind off what was probably in it. How'd he keep the garlic out of that?

"Damn," Jamie said suddenly.

"What is it?"

"I meant to stop by the dry cleaners this morning. Well, if I go first thing tomorrow you can still have your tux back for New Year's Eve."

Jamie got out his notebook, made a note.

"Oh God. Don't remind me. The Hawkes Enterprises New Year's Eve Ordeal. I dread it. It's not as if we didn't get our fill of one another yesterday. And I assume Richard's invited a hundred people."

"Two hundred, between him and Lydia. And that's not counting Rick and Barbara's friends."

"Yes. Rick and Richard are already quarreling about the music. Both have hired bands. Of course, Lydia wants an orchestra . . . By the way, I can't imagine how Richard felt this morning. Or Barbara, either. I'd forgotten how potent port can be. . . . What are you doing New Year's, Jamie? A party with the bowlers?"

"Got a date. Dinner-dance at the inn. New first-grade teacher."

"Surely not some child just out of college?"

You're the one who likes chasing after young stuff, Jamie thought, but didn't say it. He would kid around with Grenville but was never disrespectful.

"No, she's thirty, divorced, one kid. Just moved here. Miss Maples's younger sister."

Grenville raised his brows.

"Naw," Jamie said. "Emma's cute. Dark hair and eyes. Really built. Good sense of humor. It's not our first date."

Jamie had gone ahead and booked the whole package at the inn, which included a room. It wasn't any sure thing . . . just a feeling, a nice kind of suspense, like "Let's just see what happens."

He knew she felt the same.

"Grenville," Jamie said, "skip the party."

"What?"

"I mean, it's great you're so close to the family and all, but you just saw them. You're not a big party kinda guy, everyone knows that. Just take Louisa to dinner or something. Nobody'd mind."

"Several of our business associates will be there. They'll expect to see me. Lydia's charity board members too. The Hawkes Foundation for the Homeless. I can't very well let Richard represent us. And everyone's made such of point of it. . . ."

It always pissed Jamie off, the way the Hawkeses had snubbed Grenville for so long, then turned to him for money, financial advice, and finally expected him to solve everyone's problems—running Richard to the detox clinic twice a year, handling Lydia's messy second marriage, helping Rick choose a college, and not only hushing up most of Barbara's scandals, keeping her from creating new ones. And now he was the one they wanted to uphold the "Hawkes image."

Lazy snobs, Jamie thought. He didn't think he said it, even though Grenville answered, "Well. They're *my* lazy snobs, and I must do what I can."

"Okay, look, go to the party for an hour, shake hands, make sure people see you—make Louisa wear that green thing that shows her legs—you know which one I mean?"

"Yes."

"Then cut out. They won't care."

Grenville looked thoughtful.

"You see a glimmer of intelligence in my inept logic here?"

Grenville was forced to smile. "I'll think it over."

"You going to have dessert?" Jamie asked.

"No."

Grenville rarely had dessert. That's probably why he was still as lean as he'd been ten, eleven years ago, Jamie thought. His erect, commanding posture gave the appearance of being younger than his years. The lines in his face had deepened but not multiplied; in repose his face was grave, almost severe. His hair had gone a dark iron gray, with a strange sheen to it. Still a handsome man, formidable, aristocratic.

Jamie ran a hand through his own hair. It had darkened to a caramel color but was just as thick and plentiful as ever—you could count the gray hairs on one hand. The mustache he'd grown a few years ago had come in one shade darker.

It was nice to have something left to be vain about. He was well aware he was putting on more pounds each year, he'd needed glasses to read the menu.

Sighing, Jamie ordered coffee instead of pie.

"Grenville?"

"Please, no more landscaping talk."

"No, not that. I just liked the way you introduced me to Mr. Graystone."

"Jamie, I know of no more appropriate appellation than 'my friend.'" Grenville signaled for the check. He glanced around the room. Nervously, he drummed his fingers.

Jamie stirred the second spoonful of sugar into his coffee.

"Meant the 'James' part."

"Oh," Grenville said.

Jamie kept his eyes down. Grenville hated to be laughed at. There was only one thing he dreaded more . . .

"Don't worry," Jamie said. "I'm not going to cry."

———

It was silent on the way back. A peaceful silence. Once they got off the interstate onto the two-lane highway to Hawkes Harbor, they rarely passed a car.

The clouds had parted—the light of the half moon reflected from the snow. Between the dark fells of woods, the drifts of white snow were oddly reminiscent of the ocean, like swelling, immobile billows.

It made Jamie remember nights, far out to sea, standing at the railings, smoking, feeling the wind, watching stars, sky, waves, listening to the pulse of the engines, the rhythm of the water. It was like that now. Grenville, going over his contracts in his mind, would probably not say a word until they reached Hawkes Hall.

Jamie thought briefly of the book, gift-wrapped, in the trunk, then started planning how he'd insulate the pipes tomorrow . . . he'd start in the kitchen . . .

The windshield suddenly went black and shattered like a bomb had hit it. Badly startled, driving blind, he lost control of the car and felt it shoot off the road. He knew they were headed straight for the tree line . . . he made a desperate stab at the brakes—

The goose-down quilt was surprisingly heavy. It weighed down on him so much it almost hurt.

Jamie turned his head, trying to see the time.

Grenville was looking down at him. Jamie just stared back, surprised.

"Please lie still, Jamie. Another driver stopped a few minutes ago, he's gone for help. There should be an ambulance soon."

Jamie realized the weight was Grenville's heavy coat. And somewhere, Jamie was in pain. For a moment, he almost panicked.

Jamie was still terrified of pain; he couldn't tolerate it in the least. But this was different. More like a heavy pressure, really, like being caught in a giant vise.

Damn, he thought, if I've messed up my other shoulder . . .

"We're not near the shoreline, here?"

"No, it's miles away."

"Funny. I thought I heard . . ." Jamie tried to figure out what had happened.

"You hurt?" he asked, pulse jumping—there was a trickle of blood on Grenville's temple, another on his chin.

"No. Just shaken."

Slowly, the world took shape. The winter night, the snow, the cold. The car, crumpled into a tree, the driver's door thrown open, the body of the deer limp across the hood.

The massive oak he lay against. Stars. Lots of stars.

Jamie shifted, feeling a pain somewhere.

"Jamie, you must be still."

You don't control me anymore, Jamie thought. I'll do what I fucking want.

But he lay still.

Jamie could remember cold like this only once before—lying on the floor of a secret room in a long-forgotten cave . . .

But this time he wasn't afraid.

This time there was a source of warmth somewhere. He realized Grenville was clasping his hand tightly.

He tried to return the pressure.

"Your hands are warm these days, Grenville."

"Yes."

It seemed impossible that the dark eyes that met his could be the same ones that had glared up at him from the coffin. . . .

"It's been a strange trip, huh?" Jamie said drowsily. Maybe he could sleep until the ambulance got here. "A long way from where we started."

"Yes."

Jamie looked at the car. It hurt to see that car like that. To-taled. Grenville would finally have to spring for a new one. Bet that would piss him off . . .

"Look in the trunk," Jamie said suddenly. "Before it gets towed. There's a book . . ."

"Yes. I will."

(But he didn't. Grenville forgot all about it. When the auto-salvage delivered it to Hawkes Hall one week later, he stared at it for a full minute before he realized what it was. When he read the inscription, he cried.)

The vise seemed to tighten a fraction, and Jamie caught his breath. The handclasp tightened, too, and Jamie thought: I'm okay. It don't get any worse than this, I'll be fine.

Then, for the first time in many years he had a memory of his childhood. He and Colleen, they were on the ferry to Stan-ton Island, just to ride it. It must have been his birthday . . . yeah, it was June, they were eating ice cream. He remembered her flat white shoes, polished carefully over the scuffs on the heels and toes. He was jumping around, pointing at the different boats, the ones he'd like to sail on.

"You mustn't go off and leave me, Jamie."

"But I'll be back."

"And you mustn't make promises you can't know you'll keep."

He'd looked up at her, puzzled, she so rarely scolded . . . he saw it different, now. And not long after she'd broken a promise of her own . . . how angry it had made him . . .

Then it seemed like his life collapsed like a folding telescope, from that moment to this, there were only seconds in between. . . .

It goes so fast, he thought, they don't tell you that, how fast it goes . . .

He seemed to see Grenville in a rising mist. He blinked, felt the hot streaks on his face turn to cold. He saw him so clearly now.

"No regrets, Grenville," he said.

Grenville didn't, or couldn't, speak.

A twisting pain shot through Jamie's arm, exploded through his chest. Before he could cry out, he felt a finger brush his forehead . . .

"Jamie!"

Jamie realized he should have been surprised to see Kellen Quinn, but somehow, he wasn't.

"Kell?"

There was Kellen, tall and jaunty, looking like he had in the old days, full of energy and plans and the promise of great things just around the corner.

He was happy, brimming.

"Yes lad, it's me, I've come for you. There's extraordinary places waiting, a fortune beyond explaining."

He reached for Jamie's hand, and pulled him to his feet.

Jamie braced for the pain but felt none. In fact, even the small ripping pain that had plagued every breath he'd taken for the last few years was gone.

He and Kell hugged each other tightly for a moment.

"So you finally made it big?" Jamie laughed.

Kell looked great, entirely without the shifty, hunted look he'd sometimes worn before.

Kell's face sobered for a minute. "I went through some perilous times, lad, very dark weather indeed. But somehow, love of God, I made it through. And now I've come back for you."

"I appreciate that, Kell, but . . ."

As good as it was to see Kellen again, Jamie would not get mixed up in more of his scams. He was through with that stuff.

"No, Jamie, no cons this time, no tricks, it's the real thing. The real, legitimate thing."

"Yeah?" Jamie said, wonderingly.

He could see Kell was telling the truth. It felt natural to fall in step with Kell, felt good to hear his voice.

"Yes, the candles in Hawkes Hall worked fine, lit with a sincere prayer, they were just as good. It was clever of you to think of it, lad, I owe you."

Jamie felt a tug of some kind; he turned to see Grenville kneeling in the snow beside a body.

Not another one, Jamie thought in dismay.

"And I've come on a fine ship, Jamie, the best you've ever sailed. We'll pull anchor soon. Come, Jamie, it's time."

Jamie looked forward and saw what Kell had promised—a clean ship anchored on a gently rocking ocean, light glittering on the water.

"A schooner, Kell?"

"Yes, and I believe you know our captain. We're promised smooth voyages, the wind at our backs all the way. You've had your stormy weather, Jamie. It's clear passage for you."

The ship was a beautiful sight, and Jamie picked up his step. The sunlight was pleasantly warm, and he shrugged out of his coat. He didn't need it now.

I bet I can swim to that ship, he thought, with overwhelming joy.

From far behind him, he thought he heard a strangled cry.

"Jamie!"

He'll have to do without me, Jamie thought, not looking back. And then clearly, as if he'd been told, he knew Grenville *could* do without him. There was somewhere else he had to go now, somewhere else to be.

He had never seen such a soft golden light.

It lay like a path on the sea.

About the Author

S. E. Hinton was the first author to receive the Young Adult Services Division/School Library Journal Award for Life Achievement, and has received numerous other awards and honors. Her gritty and powerful novels have also inspired four major motion pictures. She lives in Tulsa, Oklahoma.